Endpoint

by Rejean Giguere

REJEAN GIGUERE

Endpoint
by Rejean Giguere

Second Print Edition - 2020
Copyright 2013 - Rejean Giguere
ISBN 978-1-927047-15-6
Ontario, Canada
www.rejeangiguere.com

This book is a work of Fiction. All characters and events (and some places) are products of the Author's imagination.

REJEAN GIGUERE

Other Books by Rejean Giguere

DreamWeaver
Merlin 444
Franklin Asylum
Jackfish Reborn
Raildogs
Woodsrunner
Mauwee Nibi
Cult of Kota

www.rejeanguiguere.com
@RejeanGiguere

ENDPOINT

This book is dedicated to my Aunt and childhood friend, the late Sherry Harvey, and to all those she loved.

an endpoint is the entry point to a service, a process, or a queue or topic destination

PROLOGUE

Chantal stood at the door, one hand on her hip, the other hand holding up a cigarette, a small trail of smoke rising upwards. No smoking laws for her. Now there was another look he'd seen before. Her head cocked slightly to the side, the raised eyebrow saying it all. *Are we done yet?*

Gary hid a grin and headed towards her. She was sexy when she was mad, but she didn't need to know that. Besides, it was an extra bonus whenever he got her going. She'd agreed to come all the way down from Manhattan to Brooklyn for the meeting so he figured he ought to get her back now that it was over. "Come on sweetie, it wasn't that bad was it?"

She didn't even answer; she took a drag on the stick, turned on her heel and stalked out the door, putting a little extra emphasis on the strut. She didn't know it, but it was this type of stuff that made her so damned sexy when she was mad.

Gary followed her out the door, grinning from ear to ear.

CHAPTER 1

Chantal pushed open the door at the bottom of the stairs. Turning left, she headed along 50th Street's mix of shops and homes. Everything from delivery trucks to motorbikes were parked along the curb. Patches of light and shadow broke up the sidewalk under the trees. Gary was a few feet behind her, lengthening his steps to catch up when all hell broke loose.

As Chantal's heels clicked against the concrete, a shadow stepped out from behind a tree, falling in behind her. The guy was between them now. Gary started to speed up, trying to get to her as the guy lunged forward and grabbed her around the neck. At almost the same instant, he saw another attacker lunging from where he had been crouching between a pair of cars.

Changing course, he headed for this new threat. In the back of his head he knew Chantal could defend herself, at least until he got there. Time slowed, his mental training took over, he kept walking forward, knowing it would take about four more steps to intercept. He glanced over to see Chantal drop down, pulling on the attacker who had his hands around her neck. Using her assailant's own momentum, twisting, she sent the guy over her head towards the pavement. Gary focused on the second attacker who had changed direction and was now coming towards him.

The guy looked big and carried himself confidently. Wading in, he threw a left jab. Gary didn't hesitate, or move back. Instead he stepped forward, inside the punch, simultaneously grabbing the guy's arm by the wrist, gripping a handful of jacket, and pivoting his hip into the thug's stomach.

Gary already had the guy off balance, and just like Chantal, he dropped down, and using the man's momentum, kept him going right over top. Unlike Chantal, Gary wasn't kidding around and while the guy flew towards the pavement, he shifted his weight again, getting a solid grip on the attacker's arm, he lifted upwards with a sharp motion as the guy fell. The crack, pop and scream were simultaneous as the guy's shoulder dislocated and his arm broke, leaving the man groaning on the street.

Now Gary took the time to look for Chantal who was circling with her attacker. The guy looked a little more cautious now. *Good girl, you're buying some time.* A commotion behind them caught his attention and he swivelled to look.

The tough-looking black dude who had been at the meeting they had just left was fighting another attacker about twenty yards to the rear. *What the hell was going on?* Gary started processing information as he headed in Chantal's direction. This was a crew, these guys were big and strong, organized.

Who was the black guy from the meeting? And what side was he on? Gary had just barely noticed him sitting off to the side at the migraine support group.

It seemed like this crew was after Chantal. No matter, it was stopping here. Her opponent had her down on the concrete and was trying to wrestle with her from above. Gary never broke stride, coming in with a hard driving knee into the guy's ribs.

The force lifted the man right off Chantal and sent him tumbling across the filthy sidewalk. Gary was right there, following. As the attacker stopped rolling, he came up holding a gun. Gary froze as his brain tried to catch up. Guns? If they had guns why wait until now? Why not pull them at the beginning? Something was off here, but there was no time to work on it, he needed to disarm this asshole.

Just then, a black van squealed to a stop. Men jumped out the side door as the driver yelled at the gunman who was staring Gary down. He recognised the language. Russian. *What the hell?*

Gary saw the attacker turn his eyes towards the van's driver, and used the opportunity to take two quick steps forward, coming up inside the gunman's arm. One hand grabbed the wrist holding the gun, while his other elbow swung hard, hitting the guy solidly on the jaw, leaving him dazed. Before the guy fell backwards, Gary wrapped both hands around the wrist. As the attacker fell, his wrist snapped backwards, broken. He squealed and the weapon dropped to the concrete.

Gary kicked the gun down the sidewalk and looked around. He felt his heart pounding and knew while he was in full gear, everything was still moving in slow motion. He watched more men coming from the van in a run, the driver climbing out, blaring orders. The black guy from the meeting seemed to be looking at Gary expectantly as he leaned over his beaten rival, pinning him to the ground. Lastly, he saw the shock on Chantal's face. It was clearly time to go.

"Run!" He pushed Chantal towards the dark space between two houses before grabbing her hand, taking the lead. He had no idea what was going on, but was sure they would lose this battle if they stayed on the street. Since he didn't know how many more attackers there were, running up the sidewalk made no sense.

*****

"What's going on?" Chantal yelled. Gary wasn't answering and that wasn't a good sign. *Jesus Christ, what the hell was going on.* Suddenly they were in the alley between the two buildings. She was agile but he was really pulling and she fought to stay upright.

Grass below her feet meant they were in a backyard. He didn't slow down, just kept dragging her into the darkness behind the house. When he stopped and turned, pointing to the high fence. Grabbing her around the waist, he lifted her up, "Over the fence. Go!" She kicked into gear and found the top of the fence, pulling herself up and over.

She didn't have to wait long, Gary dropped down beside her.

"These guys aren't fucking around, we give it everything. Right now."

Chantal jumped up and ran with him.

He was going to save her again, which was crazy, because that was how they'd first met.

A couple years before she'd made the mistake of stepping out the back door of a bar to have a smoke instead of going out the front. Some real assholes were hanging out there and next thing she knew things were getting out of hand. One of them grabbed her ass and she'd pulled away. Then another had tried to corner her, "Come on baby, we'll be easy on you. You don't want to get hurt do you?"

She'd started running towards the street, but one guy was on her pretty quick, yelling, "Hey guys, give me a hand here, we can't let her go yet." He caught her, laughing as he wrapped her up in his arms and picked her off the ground. Chantal bit his hand and made sure she landed on his feet when he dropped her. By then the others caught up and they'd swarmed her. That was when a guy walking past the end of the alley heard her scream. He'd been just walking by, but his timing had been perfect.

Chantal had seen him stop and turn. He'd taken half a second to realize a woman was in some sort of trouble. He didn't hesitate, running between the two buildings. Her attackers took one look at him, tall and slender, and seemed to think he was going to provide a little bonus entertainment. One of them held Chantal while the other two moved towards the intruder.

She watched him take on the two assholes and hurt them both. One was left nursing a couple broken bones, while the other was up against a dumpster, out cold. When she felt the grip on her arm ease, she chopped down on the guy still holding her and broke his hold, running towards the man who'd just saved her. The third guy wasted no time running the other way down the alley. Suddenly it was just the two of them standing there.

"Hi, my name's Gary, Gary Collins."

He'd been so calm that night, and every other night for three years now. But back then it amazed her how someone so calm could unleash such devastation; it still amazed her today.

They ran past the front of a house and straight across the road, around the back of another. Chantal knew that Gary had seen the van the same time she did, as it slid around the corner of the street and tried to cut them off before they crossed. *Not this time asshole*, she thought. Gary kept pulling her along as he swerved around things, jumping small obstacles.

In the next backyard they turned left and ran towards the neighbor on the side instead of climbing the back fence. Again, they scrambled over the top of a six-foot brick wall into a garden. Before she could stop to catch her breath, Gary landed beside her, "Go!"

He motioned, and away they went again. They heard someone hit the wall they'd just cleared. Chantal was in the lead now, vaulting herself over the small wooden fence of the next yard. She didn't look back, making a direct line for the next fence.

Gary caught up and silently pointed back out towards the road they had just crossed. Ducking between the cars along the curb, they quickly looked both ways before running back across the street and into yet another back yard. Chantal saw the logic, double back, the van would be one street away expecting them to continue that direction. Turning back ensured the van was out of the picture momentarily at least. They could see the guy following them on foot had figured out their plan as a tall long-limbed, figure in black started across the street on the same line.

"Keep going over fences in that direction until I catch up." Gary gave her a small shove and she didn't hesitate. The first fence was small enough to clear easily. Then she heard Gary and the attacker start fighting as she ran across the yard. The next obstacle was a brick wall. She jumped up and caught the edge, then kept working her feet on the wall until she was able to grab more of the top. She took a quick look back before she dropped over the wall, seeing a dark silhouette coming across the yard after her.

Was it Gary? It better be. She was already scared. The next couple of fences were small enough that she didn't slow down. When the person chasing her was close enough to reach out and grab her, Chantal turned to defend herself, only to be tackled back onto the grass. She was about to start kicking and punching when she heard his voice.

"Hey there sexy don't be so feisty, we don't have time for that kind of stuff. "

"What the hell are you knocking me down for?"

"Because you were going to hit me. Am I right? Well, I just did it gently. You weren't going to be so careful. Now let's sit here a second."

She wanted a cigarette, could feel a migraine coming on, and what did he want to do? *He wanted to sit a minute.*

*****

Gary knew they couldn't keep running through backyards. It was time for the next course of action. They'd created separation, now they needed to lie low somewhere. Since they were near the bottom of Brooklyn and he didn't know the area, he wasn't sure where to go. They'd come down from Manhattan to South Ferry, and then across the mouth of the East River. In Brooklyn they'd come down the Culver Line right into Coney Island, and then walked a short way to the meeting. They were well off track now.

He needed to orientate himself, figure out where he was, and where the closest transit station was. He could see Chantal was a little rattled, but hanging in there. That was okay, he was too. Silently, he motioned for her to follow as they headed towards the street, stopping between a bush and the fence dividing the next property.

"We'll wait here for a bit, okay?" He could tell that it wasn't okay by the look on her face.

"Here? Are you for real?" she whispered.

He wasn't sure. He wanted to let time go by, hoping the attackers would have to spread out their search zone. They weren't going back towards the meeting place, or the station they'd gotten off at. He wanted to head away from the meeting site, and out of the containment circle. Time was his friend. So they sat.

He was feeling a bit guilty, because the migraine meeting had been his idea. He had hoped that listening to other's symptoms and descriptions of their auras and headaches would be helpful for Chantal. He had learned a lot of new things about how migraines worked by listening to the others, like the one who said his headaches started as a slow pulse in the back of his neck, pushing up into his brain, settling a throb in his right temple. Then the throb increased until it was like an ice pick stabbing into his brain.

A long half-hour later he got what he was waiting for. A black van turned the corner of the block and came slowly down the street. Gary pulled Chantal under the bushes with him. He listened as the van rolled by and felt Chantal's fingers sinking into his arm. Okay, the attackers cleared this street and would be off to the next. He kept the two of them there another fifteen minutes.

Without a word, the pair of them started walking south. They were fully alert as they neared the end of the block. Once across the street, still walking south, it was hard to ignore the urge to keep looking back. Reading the Russian writing on the signs above the stores Gary realized they must be getting close to Brighton Beach, a well-known Russian community. He had a number of thoughts at once. He might even have a plan.

Watching the storefronts, he searched for something, finally finding it on the next block. The sign would mean nothing to Chantal but Gary translated the Russian, "The Old Man's Hole". A bar would do just fine.

CHAPTER 2

Chantal was totally confused when Gary stopped in front of a dingy bar and pulled open the door. What the hell was he doing now. *Christ, hasn't this been enough for one night.* She stepped into the bar and went from darkness to into blackness.

This wasn't like any bar she was used to. Where were the lights and loud music? This place was all dark, tiny lamps lit small tables where men huddled in the shadows. You didn't even see the unused tables if the lamps weren't lit. No one sat at the bar along the back. She wondered where the bartender was.

She stopped next to Gary, then jumped when something moved beside her. The man standing there in the shadows seemed to be a waiter. Chantal watched as Gary spoke to him in a foreign language. The waiter turned and led them to one of the small tables near the back, switching on a little lamp before he wandered away.

When Chantal sat down she couldn't see Gary's face, just his chest and neck. It reminded her of an old black and white mobster movie.

She looked at the table next to them and noticed at least two heads were turned her way. *Jesus, this place is supposed to be safe?*

"Gary, what in the hell are we doing in here?" she leaned forward, whispering.

"I need to think."

"In this place?" He was so goddamned calm that it irritated her, but he was deep in thought so she let him go. The waiter came and before she could open her mouth, Gary answered. All she understood was Vodka. Well, that would do and she settled back in her chair. She took a deep breath and realized she was smelling tobacco. Looking around she saw the odd glow of red tips in the dark. Thank god. *Think all you want Gary.* She started fishing in her purse for a pack.

"What language were you speaking?"

"Russian."

Chantal was going to have to ask more questions about this Russian thing. Back when they started dating he'd mentioned living there or something, but not much more. The waiter was obviously the bartender too, setting shot glasses of vodka on the table. Chantal slapped the first one down, wanting to calm her nerves. She sipped the second and had another cigarette while she watched Gary do his thinking.

She shouldn't have let him talk her into going to the dammed meeting. Through the whole thing all she could think about was what a waste of time it was. She couldn't wait to get out of there. But she could tell that he had been in to it, he'd even gone up to speak to the doctor after it was over. Analyzing, calculating and digesting, wasn't that what he said one time.

Now it was like he was making a decision, she could see the struggle on his face. He seemed to be wrestling with his next step. She knew he'd finally made a decision when he finished his shot, smiled at her, and waved the waiter over with a couple more.

He got out his cell phone and looked through his contacts. She saw the brief moment of hesitation before Gary finally dialled.

*****

The number had been with him for ages. Even when it changed over the years, he was always notified. He'd never called the number, and hadn't seen its owner in twenty years. The last time it changed was to a New York exchange. He wished he didn't have to call it now, but after thinking about it, and taking into account the danger that was clearly there for Chantal, he knew what he had to do.

Someone answered the phone in Russian. "Ya, kto tam?"

"I want to speak to Ivan."

"Ivan, Ivan who? Who is this?"

Gary wasn't planning to play games, "Look, I'm only going to say this once, I need Ivan Petrovski. Now. You tell him Gary is calling."

He knew the Russian would be confused, the man's job was probably just to screen calls. He wouldn't want to compromise his boss, but would definitely not recognise this caller. The fact Gary had dropped Ivan's last name would be the clincher, this Russian might not even know it himself. The guy would become concerned about doing the wrong thing with someone that knew Ivan personally.

Finally the Russian muttered, "Wait a minute."

*****

Ivan Petrovski sat in the back of one of the many buildings his numbered company owned. The Sambo martial arts training centre fronted onto the street. In the back, through a guarded door, there was an open warehouse with a training area to one side. Workbenches took up the left side. The centre was left open for the few trucks parked there.

Ivan had become a criminal while a youngster in Russia. He'd worked his way up through the neighborhood gangs and then into the Russian mob before leaving during the breakup of the Soviet Union. He eventually settled down in the Russian section of Brooklyn. Fifteen years later his fingers were into everything in this section of town, his enterprises stretched out across parts of the U.S. and back to his homeland.

Tonight he was relaxing, watching two of his men train while he played chess with another. He ought to go home to either his wife or girlfriend early tonight, but he always enjoyed the camaraderie of being with his men. Shifting his focus from the chess board, he called to one of the men training, "No Nickolas, don't twist and try to throw. You must throw and then twist. Try again."

One of his guards let in a man carrying a phone who headed right for his table. Ivan didn't like interruptions, that's why he didn't carry the phone himself. He took a reading of the messenger's face, the man wasn't supposed to come in unless it was important. His look was one of confusion.

"This better be important, because I don't have the time." He reached forward and moved his knight.

The messenger leaned much closer than usual and whispered. "The man on the phone said his name was Gary. He said your last name was Petrovski, which I cannot confirm sir."

The mention of his last name was concerning, with reason. It wasn't a name known in America, he had made sure it was untraceable. But the second that he heard Gary's name, he was intrigued.

Gary Collins – well – it had been a long time. He felt the adrenaline start trickling into his veins. Whenever Collins was around things always got interesting. The two of them were like lightning rods.

Ivan waved everyone out of the room. He poured himself a shot from the open bottle of Vodka beside the chessboard to help clear his thoughts before he raised the phone to his ear.

"Ivan here." He answered in Russian.

"Gary Collins. Is it a bad time?"

"For you, an old friend, there is always time." He was extremely curious. He didn't know what this was about, and any contact from the past could go either way. "Although I wish this was a call to catch up on old times, I assume you're calling for a reason?"

"I need your help. I wouldn't call unless it was urgent. I think I'm in your neighborhood and I'm being followed."

Ivan could hear a note of stress in his old friend's voice, but there was also the calmness and clarity he remembered. He knew Gary could handle himself, and wondered why he needed help. Then he wondered who was chasing him and why.

"The Gary Collins I knew wouldn't be needing much help. What's going on?"

"That's the problem. These people aren't after me. They're after my girlfriend. We were on 50th Street trying to get back to the subway when a professional crew, with a van and five or six Russian-speaking toughs, tried to grab her. I decided to run when they showed their hardware."

Ivan wasn't expecting that. Gary was only asking help for the woman, he didn't want her hurt. Five or six men with guns really were too much for any unarmed man. His friend was lucky to have gotten away.

"What do you want me to do?" He knew that if Gary was on the phone, he already knew what he needed.

"I don't know what business you're in these days, but I assume that you have some muscle. Can we get an escort to the B train?"

That was probably an easy assumption. But this was a simple request. It didn't sound like there was anything here, just a bit of help required. "Of course. Tell me where you are, and my men will come and get you. Tell them where you want to go and they will take you. They can even drive you home if you wish."

"A ride to the train would be a big help Ivan. Thank you." Gary nodded over at Chantal. "We're at The Old Man's Hole, a small bar south of 50th. Do you know it?"

Ivan was impressed, he knew the bar. It was a smoky side-street place where older men discussed business deals. It was a good place for quiet meetings and a good place to hide in the darkness.

"Yes, I know where it is. I'm in the middle of something important right now," he moved a pawn, "but I do want to know more about these Russians you ran into, so please fill in my men when they get there."

"Okay, but you make sure your men announce themselves when they approach, we're not kidding around here."

Ivan heard the warning and understood the danger to his men. He knew exactly what Gary could do. "Okay, they're on their way. I hope I can help. You owe me a dinner for this you know, so I hope to see you soon."

"Thanks Ivan, I just want to get through the night. I do owe you one, take care."

Ivan slowly closed the cell phone and stared at it for a moment. Shaking himself out of it, he jumped off his chair shouting towards the front of the building. As men came running into the back room, he started issuing orders. He gave the senior man specific instructions. Then he watched as his crew geared up, loaded a truck and left through the garage doors at the back of the building.

*****

Gary looked around the bar, they weren't getting much more attention than when they first came in. He knew the men were looking at Chantal. That happened. With her long legs and long black hair she was hard to miss. They both relaxed. Chantal had another cigarette and a couple of shots. He downed his own shots with the comfort that came from knowing a plan was in motion.

Now he had time to review the earlier meeting. The part that fascinated him was when people started describing auras. They seemed to settle into two types, one group had blank spots, the other had objects laid over top of their vision. He was surprised that Chantal finally spoke up at the end, describing the line she got during a migraine that ran right through the middle of her vision. It was clearly different that everybody else's.

Ten minutes later two scruffy types entered the bar. Gary's first thought was meth heads. Their dirty clothes looked like they hadn't been changed in weeks. He hoped that they didn't get past the waiter, but watched cash change hands and the two walked in. *Local dealers with cash to burn.* He eased his chair back slightly into the darkness.

The two made their way to the bar at the back of the room, coming within ten feet of Gary and Chantal's table. Everything seemed fine while the new arrivals had a quick beer and a shot. They were on their second beer and shot when they took notice of Chantal. It was possible they thought they were looking at an easy score, but Gary knew it was more likely Chantal that caught their attention.

One of them spoke up in heavily accented English. "Hey there sexy woman, you want to join with two real men for a drink?"

Gary barely shook his head, warning her not to react. Chantal kept her eyes on him. He knew she would follow his lead, she was experienced enough to be able to ignore a couple of mouthy drunks.

The cocky one decided to push it further, walking over to their table. Standing on the other side of Chantal he asked her again, "You want to come with real men? You could leave this piece of shit," he pointed across the little table.

Gary answered for her in Russian. "The next five minutes could be bad for you. Not a threat, just something to consider."

He watched the guy thinking about that. The dealer looked quickly around the room. He was calculating the danger level, and to him the potential consequences didn't seem high. He finally smiled, turning to his buddy, "Hey, this shit wants some trouble, can you believe it?"

His friend pulled a knife as he stepped towards the table, but didn't get far.

The front doors swung open and three heavily tattooed men moved in swiftly. The first intercepted the waiter coming from his regular spot in the shadows. The waiter took one look at the intensity on the man's face and stopped dead. The look was enough for the waiter, even though he had a gun in the back of his waistband. Some fights you knew to stay out of.

The second man moved directly towards Gary and Chantal's table at the back. The dealer with the knife froze, stunned to see this mobster moving towards him. The punch was brutal, sending the guy flailing backwards past Gary, where he bounced off the wall. The second dealer's voice became high-pitched and squeaky as he started talking in quick Russian, "Hey, who the fuck are you? This is my block. I run things around here."

He didn't get any further. The mobster who had just hit his buddy slammed a fist into his gut, buckling him over. He was grabbed by the collar and bent in half while he was marched towards the obvious leader of the new group. Gary had figured out that much. The last man had walked into the room while his men went to work and stood there, just inside the door quietly watching everything unfold.

When a person at one of the other tables went to get up and leave, this third one just raised a hand and motioned to the man to sit; the man slowly lowered himself back into his chair. Gary watched closely, he was sure this was one of Ivan's men. He was comfortably in control, and definitely had the room's attention.

This leader reached out and grabbed the dealer's hair as his man threw him on the floor. He pulled the piece of shit's head up and looked him in the face. "Who do you work for?" he demanded.

The dealer wasn't going to hold back, he thought the name might scare this asshole that had ruined his night out. "Bikko, I report to Bikko and he's going to be pissed when I tell him about you."

"He's going to be more pissed when I break his arm because one of the dealers he's supposed to be controlling is hassling people in bars instead of out making money. Like he's supposed to be." Tightening his grip on the guy's hair, the leader punched the guy in the mouth. The dealer's head swung back and forth as blood ran from the corner of his lips. "And you give up your boss' name so easily?" He hit the guy a second time and let him fall to the floor. Looking down at the dealer who was no longer listening, he added, "Who do you think Bikko reports to?"

He ignored his men dragging the two slumping dealers out of the bar as he finally made his way to the back corner. "Mr. Gary I assume?"

Gary was finally comfortable, this guy was on top of things. His close-knit crew were disciplined and followed orders.

"Yes, it is." Gary stood up and walked around the table. Chantal stood beside him. He stuck out his hand and gave Ivan's man a single firm, hard shake.

The guy wasn't wasting time, "We'll go now, I have a truck outside." He motioned towards the door and moved aside.

Gary pushed Chantal ahead of him, where he could keep her in his sights, and followed her out the door. Ivan's man was right behind. On the street the two idiots were gone. One of the crew was standing at the back of the SUV, watching the street, while the other opened the side door. Gary pushed Chantal into the truck and felt the leader get in behind him. The rest of the crew jumped in the front and they were moving in seconds.

"Where do you want to go?" Ivan's man was obviously clear on the plan and just needed the destination. Gary wasn't sure what to say. "We got off the F train so we shouldn't go there. What other line will get us back to Manhattan?"

The guy thought for a moment. "The B train. It's east of the F train and goes up to the top of Brooklyn then you can transfer. Okay?"

"Okay." Transferring would make it harder for anyone to follow them.

They rode in silence for a while before the mobster started asking questions, "Ivan wants to know about these men who were after you."

Gary knew that Ivan wanted to know about any men that were running a game in his area without his permission. Gary was just as interested in the answers. He recounted the events.

"… then the rest of the crew came up. They must have been watching from down the street. These guys were clearly organized and had a plan. It wasn't a great plan, but still they nearly carried it out." He went on to describe everything about the attackers, the van they used, the black they wore, and the fights that happened before they escaped on the run.

The SUV pulled up to the station and all three of Ivan's men got out. They escorted Gary and Chantal into the station and made sure they got on the train. Gary shook the leaders hand a second time as they parted, "I don't know your name but thank you. You're a good soldier, and Ivan can be proud of the work you do."

He didn't approve of criminal activities. He tried not to get involved with people in that world, but his experiences had placed him in their paths more than once. Gary understood structure so he could appreciate the well-oiled process Ivan was clearly running. He noticed the approval in the face of Ivan's man who nodded back as they separated.

*****

Gary was relieved to be back on the train heading home. What a night. The adrenaline crash left him beat. He kept reviewing the night's events and trying to piece things together. The attack happened. The question was why and who? That was too big a crew for a simple mugging. Why two random people on the street?

Then what the hell was a professional crew that size after Chantal for? She'd never been in that area before. She didn't know anybody down there. Could it be her business? Her art and photography? She wasn't rich. Neither was he, not really. He knew he might not figure it out without more information. This was nagging at him.

He couldn't believe that an innocent night at a support group meeting could turn out so bad. He wondered how Chantal was holding on. Jesus, he had probably given her a migraine instead of helping make them better.

Thinking about the end of the meeting, he tried to remember anything unusual. Methodically he went through the list of people in the room. There were only a couple kids waiting for their mother, and a hard-faced man on a cell phone who had worked his way along the back row of chairs, walking out without looking back. He must not have been waiting for anyone.

And what about the black guy who Gary assumed had been helping him by fighting one of the attackers? Who was he, and had he actually been trying to talk to Gary at the meeting?

He kept getting stuck on the fact that their attackers had guns they obviously weren't planning on using. It was only after the one had lost the fight that he pulled a weapon. Gary kept coming back to what that meant. They wanted her alive. They could have done much worse, but seemed to be holding back.

They'd only been seeing each other for three years. Was something from Chantal's past catching up to her? The sexy French accent fit cleanly with being a Canadian from Quebec. She told him she had come to New York to make it big. Gary was always amazed by people going all in and taking the big chance. He could relate, he'd done it himself.

She did have talent, her painting and photography were astonishing. Her work was real abstract stuff, half the time it left him staring at the canvas trying to figure out how she had done it. She had a small apartment downtown near her gallery. He knew she kept herself in shape. She'd been training Judo since she was in her teens, and ran a couple times a week. None of these things pointed to a past. She wasn't involved in a bunch of causes, or strange religions. Gary was pretty sure she was a great person and couldn't believe something was catching up to her.

No. Something entirely different was going on.

*****

Chantal was trying hard to stay awake. She leaned her head against Gary's shoulder as they rode in silence. Her body was coming down from the adrenaline and she was having a hard time making any sense of things. They had gone to a meeting, which she thought sucked, and then they tried to go home.

Everything that happed after that was insane. Why had that guy grabbed her from behind? Where did the other attackers come from? She hadn't seen a thing when she first stepped out onto the street. Thank god that Gary's martial arts training was on a whole other level compared to her Judo.

She reached up and probed at the tender spot where a bruise was forming on her neck. The guy had grabbed her pretty hard, which had only made it easier for her to flip him over her back. But dammit, it was going to look like hell tomorrow.

The funny thing was, she was more scared of the guys that showed up at the bar to help them than the attackers.

But then, she supposed that had been Gary's ultimate goal.

The whole Russian theme of the night bothered her. Where the hell did Gary know these guys from? Who in the hell was this Ivan guy he called? And what was their connection? One thing was certain, the guys who came to help them were surely criminals. No doubt about it. Why would Gary know those types in the first place?

She'd only known him three years, but had been sure about him right from the beginning. Had she been wrong? Was there a past that was coming back to haunt him? Jesus, she didn't need any more nights like this. Gary had told her his father had been posted all over the world to work in government embassies. Originally his father sent him to learn martial arts to deal with the bullies that confronted him at every new location. Eventually he pursued it on his own for the self-discipline and training it provided.

Chantal reminded herself that Gary was a stand-up guy and a gentleman. She was sure he couldn't have anything to do with tonight's events. Slowly, she felt herself drifting away.

CHAPTER 3

Sergi Sudnik took a long look in the mirrors of his 700 series BMW before turning off the Shore Parkway. Checking behind him – it came with the territory. More out of habit than out of necessity.

In southeast Brooklyn he eased through the streets of an industrial area that looked just like every other industrial park in the country. At the far end of a dead end road sat Septon Research. As usual, he was awed by the security surrounding the place.

The building itself wasn't much more than a midsized warehouse with a second floor of offices done in glass and steel, but it had some high-end security. The tall electric fence with barbed wire all along the top came with corner-mounted searchlights. The cameras everywhere gave the place a jailhouse feel.

At night the searchlights were so bright that when they pointed away from the facility you couldn't see the building because of the glare. Sergi was waved through rather quickly at the front gate, one of the perks that went with being number-two guy around the place. The two guards were alert, out waiting at the fence, not lazing around in the guardhouse. Nice thing about this place, there was no loose baggage hanging around, everything was well run.

In his office he started out with his regular daily routine. Even though he wasn't responsible for building security, he made it a habit to fast-forward through the previous night's feed on the gate camera.

This morning something caught his attention. He stopped the tape. There was one of his vans leaving. His night crew had gone out last night. Something had happened and he hadn't been alerted.

What the hell was going on? He was supposed to be notified when someone new was brought in. He rewound the tape and watched the black van leave the facility, noting the time, nine p.m..

Sergi played the tape forward and then fast-forward: patience was never his strong point. He didn't make it through his early years in a suffocating political environment by being patient, but by aggressively carving out a niche in the black market underworld.

He slowed the video. The van rolled back through the gates at twelve-thirty. Three and a half hours? What in the hell were they doing for that amount of time? An extraction was quick, efficient and over in minutes. There was no good reason to be gone that long.

Sergi knew he could check further, tracking down the feed from the garage where they would have unloaded from the van. Better yet, he could still catch the team leader from night shift doing a hand off to the day shift. Picking up the phone, he ordered one of his men to track the team leader down. He started working his way through the computer files, searching for the right camera feed.

He had a number of things scheduled for this morning, but this video was his only concern now. He started rolling through it on fast-forward, stopping when the camera showed the garage door opening. The van pulled in and the men exited the side door and the passenger seat. Sergi noticed that the driver sat there a moment longer before joining the others.

Suddenly he leaned closer to the screen. *What?* They were on an extraction and they didn't bring in anybody? He was confused, they only went out once a target was established. So where was the target?

He was beginning to feel his blood boil. There was no room for this kind of error. The consequences were too big. The boss was already getting impatient with the levels of success they'd been having. His anger gave way to a shiver of fear at the thought of being on the wrong side of Alexi. When a knock came on his office door, he assumed it was the night crew leader, his anger returned.

"Come in."

The man looked defeated already. That was sign he knew this meeting wasn't going to go well.

"There was an extraction last night?" Sergi's voice was crisp.

"Yes sir, we got the call and went out immediately, as per procedure."

When Sergi realized the man wasn't going to say anything else he barked at the guy, "Well! What happened?"

"Everything went wrong Sergi, we got into a fight with the target and her companion. That's never really happened before. They usually struggle and try to scream, but this time it went very differently," he stalled and then, with his head down, continued, "then they got away from us."

"This guy was able to beat your men by himself?"

"It wasn't just the male, the female fought too. She held out long enough for her companion to take out Miko and snatch her away from Sasha. Boss, this guy was a pro. Once things started he was very cool. I was watching from the van, ready to drive us out of there." He shook his head, "this guy, he took it to my men and won easily. When he saw the rest of us he made a quick decision and was gone like that."

The man looked at Sergi and realized his boss was sitting there silently waiting for the rest.

"We chased them. They ran through back yards, jumping over fences, and doubling back. We tried to cut them off on the streets with the van. Sasha got close in one yard and the man took him down hard. It was everything Sasha could do to crawl out to the street where we finally found him."

Sergi thought about it, this guy did sound like someone who had been in the thick of things once or twice. He knew how to run and he knew how to fight. This would have been a fluke. The law of averages said there was probably going to be a time when something went wrong and the target fought back. He scratched his ear, there was nothing more he would get here.

"You do understand that mistakes are not how I do business?"

"Yes sir, I would have been doing it myself if I'd have known it would go to hell like that. I can assure you there will be no more mishaps."

"Yes, you had better ensure it. There won't be another missed opportunity. You better make sure your men understand it as well. Now get out of here."

Sergi ignored the guy as he backed out the door. He had a lot to think about. There must have been someone different at the meeting last night. His teams were clear that the target had to be someone new. He could have asked the crew leader about the target, but Sergi knew he would get a better description from the sitter who was inside the meeting. He needed a coffee, this morning was taking a different turn and he had to place another call.

*****

Dr. Zolkin was glad it was Friday. He couldn't admit to anyone, but he was sick of this place. He'd signed on three years ago, all excited to work in a brand new facility. It was unique in that it was built to accommodate various types of research and had been equipped with only the best equipment.

He agreed most of the research they did here was beneficial, but one area was becoming beyond his ability to handle. Just then he heard a piercing scream. He jumped, he still reacted to it, there was no getting used to it.

Septon Research. What a mess. He knew he couldn't leave; that was obvious. He had to hope their research was successful and they would finally let him go. He hadn't understood that agreeing to all conditions when he took this job had meant living isolated at the facility. He hadn't been out of here in the last three years.

The new assistant they had just assigned to his department approached down one of the many hallways, joining him outside the most troublesome part of the facility.

Dr. Gusev was much younger and energetic than his boss. There was something about him that didn't sit well with Zolkin, but he couldn't put his finger on it. Maybe it was his eagerness to work on this particular wing of the facility that bothered him. Maybe it was that he couldn't figure out why he'd been given an assistant in the first place. He hadn't asked for one.

He had been avoiding duties on this hall as much as possible lately, but still carried out most of his responsibilities. Anything less would surely be addressed, and from what he'd seen over the last three years he knew that would probably be a bad thing.

"So Gusev you are ready to continue testing today?"

"I'm always ready, but am worried that we don't have any new guinea pigs."

Dr. Zolkin couldn't believe this guy, he wanted more subjects to test. Was the kid crazy, a psychopath? Or was he just driven to please his bosses and prove his worth?

"We don't need any more subjects. We don't need to hear any new screams either." The doctor felt a slight shiver ran up his spine, like he was shaking off the cold of Gusev's answer.

"Yes, but it's the scream of discovery isn't it?" The kid grinned wolfishly as he pushed open the door.

CHAPTER 4

Friday morning, Chantal was down at her shop early. The night before was still on her mind when she'd gotten up and quietly left the apartment. Usually her job was her escape. The act of creation allowed her to be in another world while she worked.

She had been running late on a commission and decided to bring it into the gallery to finish it. The place had begun to fill as she finished the painting. The crowd was really interested in watching her paint. At first she hadn't been too sure about it. She was a little self-conscious about being watched, but the public exposure she got working like this and the few newspaper articles it generated over the years had really boosted her business.

Chantal had become part of the art scene in Manhattan. Her paintings and photography were recognised enough that they showed up on the walls of some well-known collectors. She hadn't needed to come in this morning and was already having second thoughts. Sarah managed the business on a day-to-day basis, handling sales and appointments, so she really didn't need to hang around.

She looked around the shop and knew everything was fine. She thought about Gary at home where he did most of his work.

She picked up her bag and decided she was leaving. After speaking with Sarah for a minute or two she headed out the door.

She lit a smoke as she walked the crowded sidewalks. She'd always liked the energy and flow of people here. It had been a shock coming from Canada, but she'd settled in and become a New Yorker. She waved in reply to the hello's she received from other shop owners on her block as she passed. After nine years, her gallery was a veteran. There were only three shops on the block older than hers.

Chantal's fifteenth-floor condo looked out over the city lights at night and glass during the day. A person could see for miles from this height. She entered as quietly as she could. Gary was usually a night owl. He often worked well into the night, when his juices seemed to flow the best. She'd had a hard time when they first met and he would take her to bed, then get up afterwards and work for hours on a project. It had taken some getting used to.

She was back early enough that she hoped to find him still sleeping. Working her way through the apartment she headed to the bedroom. Opening the door, she slid silently over to the bed. Gary was still out cold. She smiled and stripped off her jeans and shirt.

Sliding her panties down and off her feet, she reached out and grabbed the silk sheet, slowly pulling it towards her. She watched Gary's chest appear and then his stomach. She pulled it down until she saw his thighs and legs. She kept pulling it until the sheet was hanging in her hand.

Wow.

The sight never disappointed her. He wasn't muscled up like a body builder, but his lean body was sculpted and taunt, even in sleep.

Chantal felt her pulse quicken and she smiled as she climbed onto the bottom of the bed, working her way up between his legs. Slowly, she lowered herself and took him in her mouth. She felt Gary wake, swelling. He moaned once and then twice as Chantal rose up and climbed on top of him.

Something about the night before had left her with energy to burn and she wasn't taking her time. Chantal slid herself up and down, pushing against him. The first pleasure was quick, the second time he joined her as they exploded. She fell forward, landing on his chest and they stayed like that for a while.

Finally Chantal raised her head and smiled. "I needed that this morning."

Gary was confused but wasn't complaining. "Anytime sexy. Thought you were working this morning?"

"I am." She was up and heading for the shower. "Did you call the cops?"

"Yeah, I did. But you didn't expect anything did ya?" Gary laughed. "They gave me the 'glad you're alright' attitude and 'if you want to come down to Brooklyn and fill out a report…'. So I don't think they really want to do anything about it."

"Seriously? Can't you call somebody else?"

"Baby, this is New York." He laughed, "muggings are a fact of life, there's just too many of them."

Chantal could go back to work now, she'd let off some steam and felt better. "See you tonight." She put her fingers to her lips and blew him a kiss.

Gary was still enjoying the moment and it took him a minute to reply, "I might be late tonight. I have something to look into."

She hesitated at the bedroom door, this happened a lot. He was always out on business or meeting people. Why that had to happen at night was still unclear to her. Gary had said that businessmen worked during the day and had their meetings at night. She would occasionally ask why they didn't have their meetings during the day like she did, but he would just laugh and tell her that these were different businesses.

She turned the water on and stepped into the shower.

*****

He spent the rest of the morning making calls and sorting out some business. He even made plans for dinner. That wasn't something he wanted to put off.

Gary was a business consultant of sorts. Over the years he'd built a reputation as a man with connections and ability to see the big picture. He was able to take smaller pieces of a problem and fit them all together.

Who would have known that the kids he'd played with in the places he grew up around the world would become politicians and government officials, businessmen, or the even more shady sort.

He found jobs or causes he was interested in, and at this stage in his life he worked on what he wanted. Mostly, he would get a call from someone asking him to get involved in a situation because he could be trusted. He had proven he could work above, around or between international lines, family lines, and dictatorships.

The fact that Gary always received generous payments for his efforts was, as far as he was concerned, just his reward for creative thought.

Right now he was trying to wrap up one of his projects. He was having a hard time focusing on the mine strike in Brazil. His mind kept going back and forth between the events of the night before and the dinner to come.

Still in his track pants he headed down the hallway to a back room, where he started to loosen up, doing some easy stretching exercises in the converted spare bedroom. Last night's adrenaline overload left him a little stiff. He needed to be loose and ready for tonight, because if there was one thing he was sure of, nothing would be straightforward.

CHAPTER 5

Taking the train down to Brooklyn wasn't Gary's idea of fun, but he'd made the phone call and this was the price he had to pay. Dinner with Ivan was payback after the help he'd received. Ivan had insisted his guys pick him up at the station and take him back later.

He walked out of the station into the early evening. The breeze felt cooler down here so close to the water. He recognized the leader of the crew that had bailed them out of the bar, "I might as well know your name."

The guy didn't look like he felt there was a need to give it, but as a courtesy to Ivan's guest he answered. "Boris."

Gary almost laughed, he couldn't tell if the guy was pulling his leg. He wouldn't put it past him. "Okay Boris. Let's go."

He sat quietly, listening to the small talk in the car. He could tell these guys were alert despite the chatter. They weren't on a social run. That was fine with him. He started thinking about Ivan.

Actually, he was thinking about the Sambo Grand Master who had made the pair of them fight that first day. He wondered if the man could have known the way the two kid's lives would eventually become entwined.

Gary's father had walked him into the dojo. They had been instructed to arrive at a time when other kids were training. With the constant moves his job required, his father felt that his son ought to be able to defend himself from the new batch of bullies that appeared at each new posting.

Not understanding any Russian yet, the fourteen-year old Gary had been shocked when his father left, saying he'd be back in a couple hours. Right from the beginning he could see the Russian kids talking about him. He was the outsider again.

He had always wondered if that first fight was to check out his skill level, or if the Grand Master had hoped he would actually beat the young Russian. Occasionally, he wondered if Ivan had been a pain in the ass who deserved a beating. Either way, he was asked in broken English if he wanted to spar. Of course he never backed down, he knew better than to show weakness at the first outing.

The dojo master didn't need to ask any of the Russians who wanted to represent the group. This one kid stepped forward right away, wanting the action. They were told to wrestle and see who could pin the other. There was to be no punching and kicking – just wrestling.

He was tall and lanky even as a kid. The Russian was short and stocky, with a confident grin, like he was going to enjoy what was coming. Gary would work on that, he was sure he could wipe the grin right off the other kid's face.

They wrestled back and forth, each of them trying harder as they realized they were pretty equally matched. The Russian kid threw the first cheap shot, ramming a knee into Gary's flank as they fell to the mat. He was hurt and went into a defensive mode, rolling out and away from his attacker. Okay, he'd thought to himself, that's how it's going to be.

The fight had gotten ugly from there on as they wrestled, rolling across the mats throwing short punches and knees. The Grand Master, realizing that someone was going to get hurt, ordered them to stop. The two boys stood up and facing each other.

He was sure that the old instructor hadn't expected things to get that heated. Now the two kids were bleeding and showing the signs of bruises. He made the two of them introduce themselves, and they both spit out the other's name.

"Gary."

"Ivan."

A relationship born of animosity had begun. He remembered staring at Ivan and seeing the blood smears from a battered nose. He also remembered that cocky grin still stretch across the Russian's face.

That was the only time they were allowed to fight in a free-for-all. Over the next four years Gary trained and competed under the Grand Master, becoming very familiar with that Russian kid, and with the levels of combat training in Sambo Martial Arts.

It wasn't a surprise when the SUV pulled up in front of a large warehouse. The front was clearly a dojo. Of course Ivan would still be heavily involved. It was like a religion to him. It had given him the tools he'd need to survive in his world, and to become who he was.

A class was in session as kids squared off against each other all over the matted room. The kids were all practicing arm moves, which was all you were allowed to do as a junior Sambist. Ivan motioned Gary to join him in the middle of the mats. Gary shouldn't have been surprised the grin was still there as they walked to join the instructor.

All around them youngsters were all busy trying to out-maneuver their opponents. Some were succeeding, while others were locked in equal battles where no one got the upper hand. Ivan pointed to the back of the room, "See this one Gary. Watch this kid."

This one was destroying an opponent twice his size. He was consistently winning the battle for arm control. Each time he got an arm hold in place he swung the other kid, who was now in a vulnerable position, flipping him to the floor.

He was a spitting image of Ivan. Fearless and ferocious. Gary laughed, "He reminds me of you at that age."

"I didn't think you would remember those first fights, it was a long time ago," Ivan grinned.

Gary laughed out loud, "Neither of us will ever forget where it began."

"You are right my friend." Ivan called out to the students, obviously the class was over. The kids scrambled to gather up their stuff and headed off to the change rooms. Ivan led Gary through a side door into his office behind the dojo. He wasn't surprised that there was a guard on the door to the hidden area.

Gary chose a chair behind the table that allowed him to see the whole warehouse. Four men trained on a smaller mat to one side, while others worked at benches along the wall. A couple attended to a pair of trucks parked inside the big overhead doors. Boris stood behind the table, facing the action.

Gary could see the age and maturity on his friend. Somehow he found it hard to imagine Ivan out doing his own dirty work anymore, but the solid look and tightness to his muscles said he could do it if he had to. Instead, it looked like Ivan had made it somewhere pretty high up the ladder.

"You look good Ivan."

"We both look good American." Ivan laughed and filled two shot glasses with vodka. He pushed one glass across to Gary. The Russian kept his other hand on the neck of the bottle. No words were exchanged, they lifted their shots, nodded, and flipped them down. Ivan refilled the glasses and they did it again. When he poured the third round he held up his glass, "To your health Gary."

Gary responded, "To your family," and then downed another shot. His head was going to hurt tomorrow.

Ivan poured two more shots and set the bottle down. The two men began to catch up with each other as they sat back drinking and watching the four men training. At some point Ivan ceased to be amused with one of the men's attitude. This one was better than the other three, and was taking advantage of them, more than helping with their training.

"Vladimir, you are too good for these three, why are you not training them? Maybe I should come over there and give you some training." Ivan shifted a bit in his seat.

"If you wish Grand Master Ivan, I can't help it if they are weak and can't master the techniques," the man said confidently.

"I think I am disappointed enough with you Vladimir that I might over-train you." Ivan glanced at Gary, "maybe you should try your skills against a simple American. Or do you only like to train with those who make it easy for you?"

"No sir, I will train with whoever you wish." The guy was looking at Gary, clearly feeling a lot better about working with him than with Ivan.

Gary knew it had to come sometime. There was a reason he'd loosened up before leaving home. Ivan had set him up nicely here, he would clear two objectives in one go.

He obviously wanted Gary to teach his man a lesson. And he had an idea which one. You were always going to run into someone better than you eventually; so always use your training time effectively, like your life depends on it. You need to understand that a team is only as strong as it's weakest link, and therefore work to improve it.

This was also Ivan's opportunity to check Gary's abilities. The two men had been apart a long time, and people changed.

"Good answer Vladimir. Please help the American with his training."

Gary gave Ivan a 'thanks-a lot' smile as he stood up. The other three men cleared out of the way, leaving the cocky one standing in the middle of the mats.

He stopped at the edge of the mat and waited for Vladimir to announce himself. When he didn't, Gary started walking directly at him. The other man took this as evidence that Gary was an amateur, so he relaxed and went on the offensive. Vladimir reached out to grab him when he got close enough. Gary stepped sideways and let the Russian's hand slide past his face, while he reached up and grabbed him by the wrist. His other hand reached up under Vladimir's armpit.

With Vladimir moving off balance, he used his own weight against him. Propelled forward by the surge, before Vladimir could react, Gary drove his hands downwards and the Russian headed towards the floor. He barely managed to get his free arm out in front to break his fall as he hit the concrete beside the mat.

Ivan burst into laughter, it was the lesson he was hoping for, "Vladimir, you disappoint me. This man hasn't even thrown a punch and here you are on your face. And what about your oath as a Sambo practitioner to always announce your status and ranking before training with a new partner? You haven't warned this man of your skill level."

Gary could tell that Vladimir was embarrassed, as well as pissed. The guy had to be wondering who the hell he was. There would be no taking it easy next time. He would be giving it everything he had.

"My name is Vladimir, I am a junior level, second rank Sambo Martial Artist. Would you like to train?" The Russian bowed.

Gary knew the system well. Three levels of specific training, within each level there were three ranks to climb. Novice with three ranks, then junior with three ranks, and senior with three more. Vladimir was middle level, second rank.

Once you were through the three ranks of the senior level you could attempt to become a master, then international master, followed by grand master and distinguished master. To advance in rank and level required beating a specific number of combatants at your own level. Each level restricted what type of combat that was allowed, progressing from arm holds as a novice, up to everything including elbow and knee strikes as a master.

Gary nodded. This time the man didn't rush in, focusing on maintaining his balance. Gary walked directly towards the Russian who wasn't sure what to do. As the aggressor Vladimir always knew what to expect. At the last second, as Gary was almost on top of him, he tried to strike out with a fist instead of reaching.

It didn't matter.

Calmly, Gary sidestepped the punch and moved forcefully into his opponent. His forearm landed across Vladimir's chest as he stepped past him, planting a leg. Gary's momentum then pushed Vladimir, sending him backwards over the leg.

Vladimir landed hard on his back as Ivan's laughter erupted. "Excellent Gary, Excellent. Come, that is enough, I think my man has learned a lesson. Besides, he wouldn't be able to work for me if I let him train with you much more."

He helped Vladimir to his feet and bowed. "My name is Gary, I am a Master in Sambo Martial Arts. It has been a pleasure to train with you."

Ivan burst into laughter as Vladimir bent forward, bowing slightly. He was more confused than ever, but relieved to hear he'd been bested by a Master and not some amateur.

"Come Gary, we'll eat now."

Gary pulled out a chair, poured himself a shot of vodka and downed it. Hopefully that was it for the physical activities for the evening, and the testing was over. He was wondering where they were going to eat when a side door opened, and a pair of women brought out trays of food. The feast shouldn't have surprised him. Things came to Ivan, instead of him going to them.

Another bottle of vodka appeared and they worked through four courses. When the food was cleared Ivan turned to his personal guard, "Victor join us for a few drinks."

For a short moment he wondered who that was. The smile on Boris's face said it all. Gary laughed, "Nice name Boris."

Victor, started to laugh as well.

Ivan let his lieutenant sit with them for an hour before asking him to take up a position outside.

The two men were drunk, but their voices were serious, even if slurred, as they worked over the events of the night before. Ivan kept drilling for information, making Gary retrace the details a number of times. He didn't care, because he was just as concerned.

"Well I'm glad you got away in the end. I wish I could catch up to this bunch and teach them a lesson for you."

"Bullshit Ivan, the lesson you want to teach them is about who's territory this is and who decides what can and can't happen in your neighborhood."

Ivan was laughing again, "You know me too well."

"Too long is more like it." Gary joined the laughter.

When the two of them had enough, they agreed to talk again later. Ivan instructed Victor to get Gary home safely. On the return trip Victor was a lot more respectful than earlier. Gary didn't notice because he was having a hard time focusing on the road.

He didn't really want to get dropped at Chantal's apartment, but was too drunk to get out anywhere else. He staggered a bit as he climbed out of the truck.

"Hey Boris, have a safe drive home," he started laughing as he stumbled towards the condo entrance. He leaned on the buzzer. "Honey, I'm home."

The last thing he remembered was feeling his pants being pulled off.

CHAPTER 6

Chantal spent the weekend and first part of the next week battling a migraine. The cold front moving in off the ocean was one of her triggers. Changes in barometric pressure sometimes sparked something and the downward spiral would begin.

She could feel it coming on, a small point behind her eye would start to pulse. If she didn't act quickly and take one of her pills, the pulsing would eventually increase. It felt like an ice pick stuck through her temple, digging around behind her eye. She would become disorientated and withdrawn as the pain increased and the auras kicked in.

If she did take her pills, she could cut off the pain, cut off the auras and leave herself a little numb and slightly slow to respond to situations. That was a side effect she could deal with. Anything was better than the intense throbbing pain.

Over the years she had gotten used to her headaches, managing to walk to work and get some things done even if she was functioning at half-speed. By Wednesday the headache was gone, and that was when Gary started in on her.

"Maybe we should give it one more shot. Especially with the week you just had." Gary was pushing to go to another support group meeting.

"I didn't think it was any good. It didn't do anything for me. Besides I don't want to go down there again." Chantal knew he was just concerned about her, and he obviously felt that one meeting wasn't enough to see if it could help her in any way.

"Why don't we find another meeting? One that's closer."

"I liked that this one was run by a professional. A lot of these things are led by support workers, but this one has a doctor." He paused a moment let that sink in, "The best thing would be for you to talk to him one-on-one after the meeting."

"I've seen doctors until I'm sick of them. Besides I already have meds that work. This whole idea about support groups is yours, not mine. I don't really think there's much sense in continuing."

"Okay, let's make a deal. This will be the last one. Go to a second meeting, talk to the man afterwards, and if that's it for you, then it's over for me as well," Gary promised.

And that was how she'd been talked into going again.

Now she was watching the city go by as they worked their way down to Brooklyn again. Night had yet to fall, it was still light out and the boroughs were still bustling, busy with cars and pedestrians. Chantal was annoyed with herself that she'd changed her mind and let him talk her into going again.

As they neared their stop she started getting nervous. She couldn't help but thinking of the way they were attacked last time. Gary had assured her that it was a one-off, they must have stumbled into something, or been caught up in some sort of mistaken identity. They both agreed that there was no reason for anyone to want to grab her and that it could only have been a mistake.

She kept an eye on Gary as their train slowed to a stop. He was calm, like there was nothing to be worried about, but Chantal was sure she could feel an undercurrent of awareness. She saw him scanning the people on the platform and all the people.

*****

Gary watched the flow of people as the train pulled to a stop. He didn't really expect trouble and mostly believed the stuff he told Chantal about one-offs and coincidences. He also knew that someone who wasn't alert was a sitting duck and deserved what came his way. Tonight, he was in overdrive.

He moved smoothly through the crowd, keeping Chantal in front of him where he could watch her as they exited onto the street. They tried to enjoy the scenery and shops as they walked hand-in-hand along the sidewalk towards 50th street. He could tell Chantal was nervous as she kept looking around.

Gary kept a good eye to the front and to the sides. If anyone came from behind he'd have to rely on his hearing. He watched for anything unusual, like black vehicles or large imposing-looking men. He was comforted that he didn't see anything out of the ordinary. As they approached the building where the meeting was being held, he slowed down a touch. He wanted time to process the whole scene.

He checked the cars lined up on each side of the street, and had a good look at the people hanging around near the building. When he was comfortable that everything looked okay, he continued towards the entrance. "Have a good meeting babe, and make sure to talk with the doc." Gary eased back and let Chantal enter the building ahead of him.

Chantal headed for the chairs at the front of the meeting room. Gary found a spot in the back like he had the last time. He waited until the session was about to start before scanning the room.

Some of the people were returnees from the last meeting, a few seemed new. He couldn't see the black guy from the other night, which was disappointing. He'd planned on talking to him. He noticed a couple of tough looking guys, but that didn't help.

The young children from the last meeting were playing quietly in the corner, and he noticed a pair of older women sat along the back wall chatting to each other. Another lady also sitting in the back looked like she belonged at the front, but Gary assumed some people came and listened, avoiding sitting up there in the spotlight.

He was trying to compare the group tonight with the one from last week, pick out the differences. Then he remembered the old guy who had been sitting at the back making a phone call on his way out the door. He looked around and couldn't see the old man anywhere. He didn't know why that bothered him.

The meeting itself progressed well. Gary listened when someone new was speaking, otherwise he spent the time thinking back to his childhood with Ivan.

Their initial relationship had been competitive. The words loyalty, respect, and courage were implanted in them at a young age. They had fought and trained like enemies in the dojo when it was time for their tests, or they were attempting to advance in level or rank.

When their dojo was in competition with one of the other dojo's they were a team, their passion to see the dojo succeed made them set aside their differences and work together, even if only temporarily.

A new person had begun to speak and Gary tuned in. The man was talking about his job. He hadn't lost it because of migraines but he was still working in an entry-level position while the people he started with were all in management.

He explained that the worst part was explaining his career to his kids now that they were teenagers and wondering about their own futures. He didn't feel successful in front of them. Gary was realizing this was another way migraines caused damage. To the family.

He let himself drift back to Russia. Unexpected events brought the two boys closer together. Gary and Ivan were always the last to leave the dojo on training nights. By this point the Grand Master was leaving them with closing duties, and the two of them often stayed long after the others.

One night Gary was last out. He locked up and started towards home. Halfway down the block he heard a commotion and looked down the alley. He was shocked to see Ivan on the bottom of a pile. He knew that Ivan ran with a rough bunch and often got into trouble. Ivan was the only kid their age that he knew who had a tattoo.

He couldn't believe anyone had gotten the best of Ivan, but then there were five of them kicking and punching him as he fought back from the ground. But what sent him running down the alley was his respect for the dojo, not Ivan. No one was going to take out one of his team. Not while he was standing by.

He hit the pile of bodies on the run, his knee-strike put the first kid out immediately, as he rolled off the pile with the air knocked out of him. The next one, who turned around at the interruption, took an elbow to the face from two feet away. He fell backwards holding his hands to a broken nose.

Gary looked down to see Ivan deliver two successive head-butts to a guy who was laying on top of him. Head butts from below, now that was creative. Gary knew that attacker was done, so he delivered a fast kick to the last one trying to pull his buddy out of harm's way.

Ivan rolled out from under the guy he'd head-butted. Gary was shocked at what came next. Ivan went nuts. He started kicking and punching all five attackers. He took them all on at once. He threw punches and elbows, and kicked them repeatedly. Once they had given up, he kept on beating them.

Finally, Ivan turned to him with that crazy grin of his, "You better leave American, it's going to get ugly here."

Gary hadn't hesitated. He'd blocked out the screams as he walked away.

He shook his head. He wasn't as focused as last week, and should be, for Chantal sake. A new woman was talking about the absentminded things that happened when she was on her medication. It cut her pain, but she didn't believe she was safe to function when she was medicated.

The meeting was coming to a close and Gary realized that Chantal hadn't spoken, but was getting up and heading towards the doctor. Gary looked around the room, back in alert mode. The little kids joined their mother up front. The two rough guys were standing.

The ladies at the back were getting up, one hung up her cell and kept chatting while they started towards the door. Gary watched them leave and then turned back to the front. There was nothing out of order.

Chantal didn't look as pissed as last week when she met him by the door, but still not overjoyed either.

"Well?"

"You're right. Dr. Killington seems like a nice guy, and a good doctor. I got his email address."

He left it at that, and they headed for the street.

CHAPTER 7

Gary went out the door first this time, checking the street. He scanned the vehicles parked along the road and looked up and down the sidewalks. Everything seemed normal.

They walked in silence past the tree where the attack had happened the week before. Playing it cool, they both stayed on high alert. Nothing happened and Gary relaxed a notch as they continued on.

This was the nice evening walk he'd imagined last week as he started pointing out storefronts, talking about the neighborhood. Chantal stopped at a small art gallery, looking through the windows at the paintings.

He talked her into a coffee and they stepped into a small café. While they relaxed, he asked about her conversation with the doctor.

"Actually, he was nice, like I said, and he did most of the talking. He told me to remember that the world of medicine is changing constantly and I shouldn't become too complacent with my meds. He wanted me to keep trying to find better and less harmful ways to deal with my migraines."

By the time they reached the station, they were both a little more relaxed, even if Gary was still carefully scanning everyone that approached them. Jogging, they beat the light before it changed at the intersection. They slowed to a walk as they started up the enclosed stairway to the station.

The sudden fog of pepper spray from all sides caught them off guard. Chantal screamed as Gary grabbed her arm. He started backing down the stairs, until he heard the van squealing to a stop. He didn't need to look back, he knew who it would be. Changing his mind, he pushed Chantal forward. He could hardly keep his stinging eyes open.

He couldn't get in front of her, or she'd be exposed from behind, so he stepped up beside her. As they tried to push through the cloud of pepper spray, Gary was hit hard on the side of the head. He kicked out straight in front of him and got nothing but air. A kick from the side hit him just above the knee, and almost sent him down.

When he turned towards Chantal's shout, he was hit from behind and fell forward, smacking his shoulder into the edge of the concrete stair. An arm grabbed him around the neck and he felt a wet cloth pushed into his face. Jesus, he was being drugged. He struggled with everything he had, looking for Chantal. A tall, skinny guy in black combat fatigues was pressing a cloth over her mouth as well.

Gary felt himself being dragged down the steps. He struggled to maintain consciousness, he was in and out, and couldn't stay with it. Upside down, he recognized the van. He opened his eyes again when he cracked his head on the steel interior wall.

He tried to keep his eyes open as Chantal was dragged into the van. He could tell she was out cold. Her body was limp as a rag doll, hanging down over the skinny guy's shoulder. He tried to lift himself and heard someone laughing. A hand pushed him back to the floor. He couldn't do anything, his body felt paralyzed. Then the van jerked forward.

Gary came to again, and took a second to brush away the fogginess. Lying on his back, with his arms pinned beneath his body, he twisted and realized he was in handcuffs. Looking around at the five men in the back of the truck, he tried to get up, his shoulders hurt from the awkward position they'd left him in.

Over his shoulder, he could see Chantal was still passed out cold. They must not have travelled far. He struggled to stay awake and take in what he could. He watched the five guys staring back at him. He didn't know that they were amazed he was awake at all. They'd never seen someone manage to stay awake while fighting these drugs. They stayed just out of his reach even though he was handcuffed.

Gary knew this was a bad situation, they'd actually come after them a second time and he still had no idea why. He knew their capture had to be important to someone, for some reason, and they were making sure they got what they were after. He just wished the drugs would let him think a little more clearly. He tried seeing into the front of the van. The guy in the passenger seat was talking on a cell phone, holding a second phone in his other hand. Gary focused slightly and recognised it as his. Shit. Of course they'd have taken it. Probably his wallet too.

He kept at the short breathing exercises and muscle control he'd learned years ago, trying to ward of the effects of a drug attack. He was still drifting in and out, and wanted to be more awake. He needed to be more awake. He felt his eyes closing again and couldn't stop it.

When he came around for the fifth or sixth time it was because of the sudden crash of steel on steel. Gary wasn't sure what was going on, but the van went sideways as the screeching escalated. He rolled across the van floor, smacking into the sidewall. The five in black combat fatigues were thrown sideways, and he realized they'd crashed the vehicle. Could it get much worse?

CHAPTER 8

Deuce had the five-ton truck roaring in third gear. The rev's redlined as his hands clenched the wheel. His passenger slid open the small door to the back compartment and yelled out a warning. They were about to hit.

He clenched his teeth and braced his back, as they slammed broadside into the black van. The accelerator stayed pinned as ripping metal screeched, while he drove the van sideways up over the curb. Deuce knew he was taking a chance he might hurt the couple inside, but he had to shake up the fuckers in charge.

Still accelerating, the truck slammed the van into the wall, pinning it to the building. Deuce was momentarily stunned. He hadn't been sure it would work, but hey-Jesus, these mothers weren't going anywhere. His boys poured out the back of the five-ton and ran towards the van. Deuce and his passenger took up positions on either side of the truck watching the street for anyone looking to interfere.

His men ripped the back door of the van open. The first Russian rolled out of the back, thinking someone was helping them after the accident. Two of Deuce's guys dealt with it by giving him a few shots to the head. They dragged him from the back of the van and dumped him on the sidewalk out of the way.

Another Russian, realizing they were in some sort of trouble was attempting to free his gun from a side-holster. Deuce's man was quicker, his bullet struck the Russian, slapping him back against the rear of the driver's seat.

With a gun stuck through the window of the passenger door, no one in the front moved. Two of the men remaining in the rear were out cold from the accident, and the third was moaning too much to be a worry.

It was clear who the captives were, even though Deuce had given his men descriptions. The cuffs were a dead giveaway. One of the men reached in and grabbed the woman's legs and dragged her out the back of the van. Then he bent down, picked her up around the waist, and easily threw her up and over his shoulder. He turned, heading quickly towards the five-ton. The last two rescuers reached in and grabbed a leg each, pulling the man out. They kept an eye on the guy who had his eyes open and was watching them intently.

Deuce supervised as the man was lifted up and put into the back of the truck beside the woman. With one last look up and down the street, he swung into the cab of the truck. His men cracked the attackers on the head a few times with the butts of their guns to make sure there were no witnesses to their escape.

Untangling his vehicle from the damaged black van, he backed off the sidewalk. Deuce could see a handful of bystanders had gathered, but luckily no police yet. He knew the truck was safe: no identifying marks, and a stolen out-of-state plate on the back. They just had to get off the block and away from the main road.

The truck surged upwards with each gear change, as they accelerated. Big black clouds of diesel smoke poured out above the truck as they took the first corner with the pedal floored, the truck shifted dangerously high on the one side as they made the turn. Everyone inside rocked from side-to-side as the truck wobbled back and forth before settling. Deuce never lifted his foot, keeping the pedal pinned to the floor.

*****

Gary's head was hurting, but too much was happening to be worrying about that. Did that really just happen? As far as he could figure, someone had crashed into the kidnappers on purpose, smashing up their van. He had passed out part way through it all, but remembered waking up as the van doors were flung open. If he hadn't already been kidnapped, he would be sure that was what was going on. Instead, something in his fuzzy brain was telling him this was some kind of rescue.

The gun that went off in the confines of the van, just feet from his head, made his ears ring as the flash blinded his eyes. These guys were serious. He didn't do anything except watch as two men pulled him out, and carried him off behind Chantal.

Now he was a lot more focused, he was starting to gain back his head. Chantal was moving a little and seemed to be waking a bit. He looked around the back of the dark truck and could almost make out the men sitting around them.

Two black guys, two white guys and a Latino. None of them looked like pros. They were all dressed differently in shirts and jeans, or cut-off tee-shirts and khaki's. Something about their casual attitude told Gary they were experienced in some way.

"So are you going to take these things off?" He looked at the Latino closest to him, motioning with his arms behind his back. The guy closest to the front of the truck knocked on the dividing door.

"He wants his cuffs off."

"Go ahead Bobby. Get the things off."

Everyone heard the answer. The Latino reached into one of the bags on the floor and came up with a large set of bolt cutters. He got on his knees and waited while Gary leaned forward. The snap of the breaking chain was music to his ears, but as he let his arms fall to his sides the pain hit his shoulders. Christ, that hurt.

Rotating his sore joints, he folded his arms in front of his chest and tried to work out the kinks. Finally in control of his arms, he reached out and took the cutters, crawling over to Chantal.

Gary gently rolled her on her side and snugged the cutters around the chain. She came to confused and scared. Waking in the dark, surrounded with men, she struck out when she sensed someone close, kicking Gary in the thigh.

"Dammit Chantal. Easy it's me. Everything's okay."

He could tell she was still confused and freaked out. Obviously she didn't know that they were now with different people than the ones who originally attacked them. She probably still thought they were the kidnappers.

"Hey girl, everything is okay. These guys just rescued us. We're safe."

Gary watched her try to comprehend, the drugs still making her confused.

"Where are we going now?"

"I don't know." He had been wondering the same thing.

He sat back as the truck rumbled along the street. He couldn't believe they'd been attacked by the same group a second time. That meant that they had been specifically targeted. He couldn't get his head around that. Why? What was the purpose to all this?

The fact that there was another group of people involved in this thing only confused the issue. He knew there was a possibility that both groups had bad intentions, but the actions of group number two seemed to indicate that they were on his side. He could push the issue and confirm it.

"I want to talk with the boss."

The kid at the front knocked again. "He wants to talk to you Deuce."

"Change places with him. I don't want him up front where he can be seen."

That was good enough for him and he whispered to Chantal to hold tight. Crouching, he wobbled up to sit where Bobby had been. If he turned his head just right he could see the driver through the small opening.

He'd thought he'd seen someone familiar when he was being moved upside down to the truck. Now he was sure. It was the black guy from the first meeting. The same rough looking guy, who had been watching him in the meeting and helped out in the fight on the sidewalk outside. Gary had really hoped to see the guy at this week's meeting, but was glad to see him now.

"Gary's the name."

The guy turned briefly before returning his eyes to the road and nodded. "Deuce."

"Okay Deuce. Thanks, I think. Now do you mind telling me what in the fuck is going on?"

CHAPTER 9

Deuce slowed the truck down and cruised up side streets, working his way into an industrial park. He wasn't drawing attention, which was exactly his plan.

Gary waited for an answer. He really did want to know what was going on.

Deuce started talking to the windshield as he steered the five-ton.

"I wish I could answer you man, but I can't. This here war's been going on for a while." He glanced back briefly at Gary, "I'm just a soldier. Dexter will fill you in better than me."

That didn't help his situation much. Obviously two groups against each other. Each organized and with soldiers and bosses on top. What the hell could he and Chantal have to do with this mess?

"Come on Deuce, you can do better than that."

"Look man, people been disappearing off the streets here for a while. We don't know how those fuckers from Septon are getting away with it. We keep fighting them and trying to save people."

Now he was intrigued. There was a name, for the first time a hint of who was behind this. Septon. He didn't know who, or what, that was, but he would be on it now. People disappearing sounded a little far-fetched, but what he'd seen so far was hard to ignore.

Gary had more questions now than when this thing first started. It was funny how that worked. Sometimes to get an answer you had to ask more questions and peel back the layers, something his business career had taught him.

"What's Septon?"

"Septon Research. It's a big wired-up place in the flatlands. People go in but they don't come out."

A research facility, now that was interesting. He couldn't wait to get to a laptop. He had enough now to track them down. Deuce had mentioned a Dexter. He obviously was above the driver in this operation; the sooner that Gary was talking to the guy the better.

"So we're driving around in circles Deuce. What's the plan?"

"I got to make sure no one is following us. Don't worry, we'll be stopping soon. It's a safe place." Deuce chuckled.

Gary realized patience was required, and shuffled back to wait with Chantal.

The truck eventually downshifted and swerved to the right, Gary felt the bump as they bounced over some sort of a curb. It sounded like the truck had entered a building as the engine noise changed.

The engine shut off and he heard the front doors open and close. When the back door slid up and the inside of the compartment was flooded with light. Gary and Chantal lifted their hands to shade their eyes momentarily. The light was bright after the darkness and effects of the drugs.

When Gary finally got focused, he was looking at Deuce waiting in the open door.

"Welcome to the underground. Glad we could help you guys out. I'm really sorry about the meeting last week." Deuce tried to explain, "I really tried to get to you before you left."

"That's alright Deuce. Your fighting that night helped us get away. What you did tonight makes up for it plenty. Thanks again." Gary climbed out of the truck and stuck his hand out.

"No problem." Deuce turned to the men still in the truck, issuing orders. "Lock up the truck and the outside doors. Wait a good hour. Make sure no one has followed. Then meet us down there." He turned to the couple, "This way."

Gary and Chantal were led out of an empty warehouse, through one office and then another. When Deuce went to walk onto a locked closet they were confused. He pushed open the back of the closet to reveal a flight of stairs, at the bottom there was another locked door. When Deuce pulled this one open, there was a sudden rush of noise and smells. Gary was shocked.

*****

Chantal was really upset. That was pretty normal when things were out of control. Right now she was hanging on tight to a run-away train. Jesus Christ, what the hell were they getting into? She had no idea where they were, or what was happening. She never should have gone to that dammed meeting.

Chantal could remember the attack. The dense fog of pepper spray had choked her before she could do anything more than raise her hands to cover her eyes. She'd heard blows hitting flesh so she knew Gary had tried.

The next thing she knew, she was waking up in a truck surrounded a bunch of strange men, while Gary was trying to tell her everything was fine. It was only after the truck had stopped, watching Gary and the tough looking black guy shake hands that she was able to believe they were okay. It didn't take long for her to get concerned again.

Chantal had a bad feeling about going down below the abandoned warehouse, but when the Deuce guy opened the last door things got a lot worse. She couldn't believe her eyes. There were people everywhere.

The large basement was open at this end. She couldn't even see the far end, the whole place was that divided up. When Deuce and Gary started walking through the maze, Chantal followed in a daze.

There were people of all ages walking around, or working on something. A few others were just hanging around at the tables in what must have been a dining area. There was an open kitchen area. A couple of women watched over some kids as they played in the corner.

All along the one wall were small rooms that looked like sleeping quarters. Chantal couldn't help thinking this place looked like some sort of commune.

She wondered if they were organized enough to have a shower in here. The skin on her hands and around her neck where she had taken a direct hit from the pepper spray was burning and itching.

*****

Gary looked around as Deuce led them through the congested basement. The abandoned warehouse on top was camouflage for the shelter. Probably gated and locked. They had tapped into electricity and water that was already there. It looked like they were pretty well kitted out with electric stoves, heaters and lights. The layout was a standard emergency field unit, food and accommodations on one side, cleaning and latrines on the other. The only thing he didn't see was a medical area. He was sure he was going to find Dexter in the rear sitting area.

Gary could see the stress on Chantal's face. He reached out and grabbed her hand, giving it a squeeze. He tried to give her a smile as she looked his way, but she gave him a deliberately blank stare in return. Deuce smiled at and waved to people as they walked by. He obviously knew a lot of the people, and must have been here a while. He was heading right for a group gathered in a corner at some tables.

When a big guy stood up, Gary knew it had to be Dexter. Not because he was by far the biggest guy, but because when he stood, everyone else turned to look. The large black man wasn't muscled up from years of working out in the gym. He got his size naturally, carrying a lot of weight.

"Dexter, here's the couple. We got 'em back from Septon. The fuckers lost big tonight."

"Everyone safe?"

"Yeah, we roughed up the Septon boys, but we're all okay."

"Alright, you guys wind down, get some food. It sounds like it was a job done well." He raised his hand up in the air and Deuce slapped the high five. He was smiling as he walked away and left Gary standing there.

Gary was thinking that he liked this Dexter fellow right off the hop. He cared about his men's safety. A good leader would always have committed men. A good leader was someone that Gary could work with.

"Gary Collins and my girlfriend Chantal Levi." He stuck his hand out once again. "Quite the set-up you have here."

He could tell Dexter was checking him out. The guy wouldn't want to say too much right away. He didn't know this newcomer and he had an operation to protect. The guy was obviously a thinker. Gary could relate, so he was willing to be patient and let Dexter go at his own pace.

"Well, it's okay I guess. It's a necessity right now." The big guy reached out his hand. "Name's Dexter"

Dexter turned and called for a woman named Mary.

"Mary, can you take Chantal here so she can clean up and sit down to relax and get some food."

Gary knew his girlfriend wasn't sure about leaving him. "Go ahead, I'll catch up shortly."

"Is someone going to tell me what's going on or what?" Gary watched the two women walk away.

Dexter pointed to an unoccupied corner table. He didn't care where they talked. He sat there quietly waiting until Dexter finally started to talk.

"Two and a half years ago my father disappeared. He'd gone out one night to a support group for people who had migraine headaches. My dad had them bad. I always felt he went missing after the meeting, so I hung out down there nights looking for him. That's when I found the others."

Others? Gary knew enough to let the man keep speaking, and continued to sit quietly.

"I ran into this dude that was looking for his wife. When he told me that she'd gone to a meeting for her head problems and never come home, I knew I was on to something." Dexter stopped like he was thinking back.

"I went to the cops, and tried to talk to anyone who'd listen. You know what? No one would. Around a year ago I met Deuce. He'd lost his sister at the same meeting. We've taken a different turn since then."

Gary had been leaning forward, listening hard. Once he realized Dexter was done, he eased back in his seat. People were disappearing from the meetings? This was obviously the connection to Chantal, but he wasn't any further ahead. Gary had his first question ready.

"Deuce mentioned Septon Research. Who are they?"

Anger flashed briefly across Dexter's face before he answered. "We started staking out the meetings and saw this rough looking crew take an old man just down the street from there. We weren't prepared to follow them that night, but the next time they grabbed a young woman." He turned to face Gary, "We followed them back to a fenced-in secure facility, and we're sure this is where all the people are being taken. I'm sorry buddy, but I don't know why they take people, or what they do with them."

"What about the police? What have they done?

"First they ignored me. Then when a bunch of us went in with the same complaint, they took a drive out and talked to Septon, but that's where it stopped. They said they didn't see anything out of the ordinary.

"When I told them we had a hundred or so people holed up together for safety they were sure we were some sort of cult, and wanted to know what we were up to. Now we go it on our own and keep to ourselves." Dexter shook his head.

Gary couldn't believe what he was hearing. It wasn't that he didn't think things like that happened, because the things he had seen in third world countries had taught him that money and corruption could move mountains, and make anyone untouchable. He had just never experienced it here in his own country.

He wondered if he shouldn't call the cops again. But then he knew he had nothing on Septon that they would believe, so all he had to report was another mugging. He also had to think of what Dexter had said, he didn't want to bring any trouble to the shelter. Chantal was safe for the moment, so he could hold off until he had something firm on Septon.

"Why are these people here Dexter?" Gary looked around.

"These people are all affected by Septon. When those guys realized we were watching the meetings and it was harder for them to get people, they just broadened their net. There were other meetings, and they started covering them all." Dexter stared at the kids playing in the corner.

"We have about thirty-five families here that have lost someone. They're too scared to go home, or don't have anywhere to go. The rest are single people we saved just like you two."

Mind-boggling. Gary couldn't believe it had gotten to this point. How was no one investigating the missing people. He knew people went missing on a regular basis, but not on a mass scale, and not from the same location. This was nuts.

It seemed that Dexter had done everything he knew how to do. He'd settled on the next best thing. If he couldn't get the authorities to stop Septon, he was going to try and stop them any way he could. Even if all he could do was work at the street level, and all he did was prevent as many kidnappings as he could.

Gary had too much going on in his head at the moment to sort it all out. He wanted to find Chantal and relax. He needed to think about this stuff and figure out what they were going to do next. "You're sure this is about the migraines?"

"They don't take everyone, just certain ones and I can't figure it out." Dexter was sure. "One thing though, you and Chantal had better consider staying here with the others, because it's dangerous for you guys right now. I'm very serious. No one has ever come back once they've gone into Septon. You think seriously about protecting Chantal."

Those words rang in Gary's ears as he thanked Dexter and went in search of his girlfriend.

CHAPTER 10

Sergi rushed back to the facility when he got the call that one of his crews had gone out. New procedures had been put in place after the last failure, and he made it crystal clear that he expected to be called when anything happened. He had been both disappointed and excited after getting feedback from a sitters at the last meeting.

The older man was one of a number of people who were paid to sit in on the meetings and watch for prospective subjects.

Initially they had taken anyone with headaches and subjected them to a battery of tests. Over time they had narrowed down the types of subjects and created a list of symptoms for the sitters to watch for.

It was disappointing to miss someone with a new symptom. They had been having a hard time getting new subjects that met their criteria lately. Apparently these new symptoms weren't even on their list. *New symptoms?* Intriguing as hell.

When Sergi got into the facility and realized the crew hadn't returned, he started to get antsy. Rushing back to the garage he stopped in at the security station to verify the time they had exited the facility. Two hours was too long.

It was exactly a week since the missed pickup. Did the couple come back? Did they make a mistake and give his crew a second chance? This woman might be the key to all their research. Maybe the end was in sight. Although he still didn't know what their end goal was. No one did. But Alexi's persistence was the driving force behind the facility, the operations, and the research. The boss would be rewarding anyone who helped him finish his project.

A call had to come in from a sitter to get the crew out in the first place, so he needed to talk the sitter from this week's meeting. The security guard looked up the number and Sergi walked down a hall searching for some privacy. Slipping into an unoccupied office he dialled.

"Hello, this is security from Septon Research. I want to ask some questions about this evening's meeting."

"Okay." The voice was hesitant. "I had been doing my normal survey and was told to watch for a specific woman. Although she didn't speak, I was sure it was her. I made the call, and then left like I'm supposed to. Is everything okay?"

Sergi knew she meant okay with her job, which was fine. She'd done exactly what she was supposed to. "Everything is fine, thank you."

He hung up without waiting for a reply. This was great news. Now he just had to figure out where the crew were.

He didn't have long to wait.

The garage doors started to open and he watched in disbelief as the van was backed through, hanging from a tow-truck. He walked around to look at the smashed-in passenger side. A taxi stopped outside and then left. His men walked into the garage.

Sergi noticed that the subject wasn't present. Surely these fools weren't stupid enough to return empty-handed. Finally the tow-truck left and the garage door closed. Sergi stared at the crew. They were nursing injured arms or legs, sporting bruises and dried blood. The crew leader, the same one from the previous weeks failed attempt, stepped forward.

"I am sorry Sergi. We had the woman and her companion when we were attacked by that black guy and his crew."

He knew who the black guy was. He'd had them tracked back when they first came on the scene. Deuce and Dexter. He had wanted to take them out back in the beginning, but Alexi would have none of it. There was to be no violence was on the streets that could bring attention. It had been hard to not kill them, but his fear of Alexi was a powerful thing. He'd been told to keep business rolling and work around them.

"You let them take her away?" That those fucking idiots were interfering with the capture of the new woman was infuriating. "First you can't get her, then you can't keep her." He stared at the crew leader. "What do I pay you for?"

"Sir, they hit us with a five-ton truck and pushed us off the road. They shot Sasha. We weren't ready for that." The crew leader described the chain of events.

"Well then you won't expect this," Sergi took two steps forward, pulling his gun out of the back of his waistband. The gun was almost touching the man's head when it went off. The back of his crew chief's skull blew off, splattering out behind him. No one moved as the room became eerily quite. Sergi shook his head, and with the gun still in his hand, turned to the rest of the crew.

"Does anyone here have what it takes to be a leader?"

No one moved. They all looked at each other and back at their boss. Sergi cocked the gun and asked again, "Does anyone here have what it takes to be a leader?"

One of the men stepped forward. That always amazed him. The question itself was enough to cower those that could never lead. But experience had shown him that a warrior could never sit back without trying. The warrior would always step forward, even though he knew the consequences of failure.

"Petrov, sir."

"Alright Petrov, you better be in the meeting with the other crew leaders. I expect you to get a handle on your men and have them better prepared than this fellow did." He waved his gun at the bloody body on the floor. "Maybe cleaning up this mess will be a good reminder to your men about the consequences of failure."

As he turned away, he felt a headache coming on. Jesus, Alexi was going to be pissed about losing the woman. Then he shivered at the thought of Alexi finding out about his own migraines, and knew that things could be a lot worse.

CHAPTER 11

Gary and Chantal settled down on a big couch. Both of them had cleaned up a bit and eaten. Chantal tried to digest everything that Gary had just told her about Dexter, his people, and Septon.

Chantal wanted to get the hell out of there and get back to the comfort of her condo. She didn't really care about this Septon. She thought they should still have the cops deal with this, even if Gary and Dexter didn't think they would get any help without more evidence. This whole sideshow seemed ridiculous to her.

"Let's get out of here, lets go home."

"I'm not so sure about that Chantal. I need to understand what's going on. You're clearly in danger, we need to weigh all our options before we do anything crazy."

"What do you mean?" She couldn't believe her ears. Options? He wasn't thinking of staying in this place was he?

"Look Chantal, they have my wallet. So that means they have our address and the contact list in my phone." He was resigned to that fact. "They could show up at our place any time. I don't think it's very safe right now. Sorry."

She let it continue digesting. She couldn't go home.

The little pulse behind her eyes signalled the first signs of a migraine. Of course she should have expected it. She fished around in her purse only to realize that it was half empty. The bastards had been through her purse too, it looked like they taken both her wallet and meds.

"I need some medication, Septon took mine. I'm going to ask around and see if anyone here has any."

"Okay, I'll be around. I want to do some research."

*****

Gary watched Chantal leave. He hoped she found some pills because he'd seen her without them, and it was ugly. She started off cranky and unreasonable, then as the other symptoms kicked in she became lost. Most of the time she would just hide in bed until her meds started to work. The few occasions that she hadn't gotten her pills in time had been brutal. He'd seen her in pain so bad she just stood in the middle of the room with tears running down her face. Once she had gotten vertigo, and ended up vomiting all over the hood of his car.

It didn't take Gary long to find a laptop and squirrel himself away.

Was he missing something? Vascular headaches are caused by the swelling of blood vessels in the nerve endings that coil around the arteries of the brain. As the swelling causes them to become bigger they release chemicals and tighten around the arteries. Those chemicals cause more swelling, pain, and further enlargement of the artery. With nowhere to go, the nerve endings tighten around the artery, the swelling magnifies the pain.

That was really pretty straightforward. You didn't want the blood vessels swelling in the first place. It caused a chain reaction that was only guaranteed to get worse. Okay, so most of these headaches were doing the same thing. Gary put his head back into the research.

He was taken back a little by the numbers. Migraines affected twenty-eight million Americans. Seventeen percent of women had them and six percent of men.

Gary had never heard of the stomach being part of migraines and realized that the whole thing was a lot more complicated than just a headache. He'd been with Chantal for three years now and should have looked at all this a lot earlier. Shit, she dealt with this all the time.

He wondered about others. He knew Chantal was in shape, intelligent, full of drive and he saw how it affected her, the days she spent barely functional, or hiding in a dark room, sleeping. What about those that were down on their luck, or unhealthy to begin with? How did you function, keep jobs, have relationships, and carry on with life. It must be hell.

Finding the right meds could be difficult because everyone was unique and reacted differently. This also explained the various reactions sufferers dealt with, because the symptoms never seemed to be the same.

Gary was looking at the symptoms online. Intense throbbing or pounding pain involving one temple – that he knew about. It could also be behind the eye or behind the forehead. It was usually on one side, but in some cases could be both.

Chantal complained that some things caused her migraines, like direct sunshine or flashing lights. It was also triggered by weather. Bad weather moving in, or changes in the barometric pressure seemed to really do it to her. The internet said hormones, alcohol, chocolates and nitrates in food could also act as triggers to the migraines.

Many people were largely undiagnosed and untreated. Most buckled down with a bottle of Tylenol or whatever they could find and rode out the pain in their own way, especially people that didn't have doctors or insurance.

He stopped and looked around. Crazy to have to deal with. There were a couple of variants to the normal migraine which caused lower brain malfunction which led to fainting and vertigo, or caused paralysis on one side of the body and blindness.

Gary kept coming back to the part about auras that included flashing lights, brilliant colors, patterns and dots. If twenty percent of migraine sufferers were prone to auras, then twenty percent of seventeen percent was – aw hell – still lots. Some of the auras created a form of blindness called scotoma. Some people had holes where their vision was blank. Others had extra shapes or patterns showing up over top of their vision. Some had one side of the field of vision missing.

Gary was sure if he had a choice he'd rather be missing a piece of vision than have extra pieces showing up. At least with something missing you could see around it and guess the missing part.

He leaned his head back against the wall. What did this have to do with Septon. What part of this were they interested in, and why? Nothing was standing out, and there were so many possibilities. Was it the migraine sufferer they wanted? Was it something to do with medications that they were after? Or a cure they were searching for? None of it made sense. Why wouldn't they just conduct regular clinical trials like all the other drug companies?

Gary asked someone passing by if he had a cell phone. The guy didn't hesitate. He stood there and waited while Gary made his call.

"Da?"

"Tell Ivan its Gary." No response, but he could hear the footsteps as the guy went for Ivan.

"Kak dyela," Ivan repeated, "*How are you?* My man saw you grabbed after the meeting. What happened?"

He wondered about Ivan's man being at the meeting, but quickly decided that his friend was just watching his back.

"This time they got us. But they didn't get far, another group of underground guys broke us out of there. It looks like the outfit we're after is called Septon Research."

"Yeah, I know. I had my guy following anyone who bothered you." Ivan explained. "He sliced the tires on a car who was observing the whole thing from a distance, and followed the first group back to their base."

"Find out what you can Ivan, I'm out of commission until we figure something out. That outfit seems serious."

"Don't worry, I can be serious too."

Gary handed back the cell phone. If it wasn't the headaches Septon was after, perhaps it was something to do with the medications. There was big money there.

Most sufferers took Tylenol and aspirin for mild cases and triptans for severe cases. Triptans attach to the serotonin receptors on blood vessels to reduce the swelling, the theory being that this would reduce the pain.

Patients with migraines that lasted for days didn't wait for the headache to start and usually just took a regular dose of something every day. Chantal had mentioned that one doctor had wanted her to take beta blockers like they gave to people with high blood pressure, and an anti-depressant medication too. She didn't want to take that kind of thing.

Gary was looking around at the people down here in a new light. He wondered who was in pain and didn't have medication. Which ones were suffering auras and seeing things? How were these people able to stay down here? And who was paying for it all?

Chantal slid her back down the wall until she was sitting beside Gary. He could see she was in a different mood. He was sure she wanted to leave, but he couldn't let that happen at this point. He was about to say something when she spoke first.

"This place is sad, these people need to get out of here. There's hardly any supplies and some of them have been here almost a year." She shook her head, "a year Gary, that's absolutely insane."

"That's why I want to stay and figure things out." She was having a headache and Gary was feeling more compassion than usual. He reached out and pulled her in closer, wrapping an arm around her.

"I'm tired," she stated matter-of-factly,

Chantal was out a short while later, and Gary was left to his own thoughts. They both had money and could live on the road for a few days. They needed to get to the bank for cards, cash and to buy some clothes and supplies, but otherwise could do it. Both their businesses would go on fine. Chantal had her manager, and Gary because he was self-employed.

It was already late Thursday night and he came to a conclusion. With the weekend so close, they could ride it out here and try to figure something out by Monday.

He had been in a number of tight situations over the years and had some close calls, but he'd usually known what he was getting into. Normally it didn't involve someone he cared for. Here he had no idea what was going on, and he couldn't let that go. This wasn't about him. It didn't matter how tired he was, he needed to keep at it. There was no way they were taking Chantal.

CHAPTER 12

Friday's weekly meeting at Septon Research was about to get under way. The managers were all sitting around the table fidgeting nervously. It was always that way when they sat in front of Alexi. At seventy-years old he could still stare down anyone in the room.

No one knew anything about Alexi, where he came from, or what his history was. But he had history. You didn't know why you knew, you just did

Dr. Zolkin was almost shaking. The Manager of Research hated these meetings. He really was just plain scared of his boss. Christ, he shook his head, if only he could go back and do that job interview over again.

The doctor had been under the gun more and more over the last few months. Alexi's patience was running out. He wanted results. Zolkin wasn't sure he was going to be able to get what his boss wanted. He didn't have the stomach for it anymore. He'd never really had the heart for it, but in the beginning the pay was just so much. What a mess he was in. The pay didn't matter anymore, but his sanity did.

Sergi leaned back, looking far more comfortable than he felt. As the Manger of Field Operations he knew that the boss would be annoyed when he found out they lost the same subject twice.

The fact that she was different from the others and represented a new research angle would really piss him off.

He didn't think he was in any danger from Alexi, but disappointing him was enough. He wasn't too happy himself. He really would've liked to have that woman inside the facility and be spending this meeting telling Alexi about the new possibilities. Instead he was going to be back-pedaling and defending himself.

Why his crews hadn't gotten the woman was also bothering him. This wasn't the first time an operation had been interrupted by those guys, and even though he was supposed to leave them alone, he'd been thinking about them all day. It was their fault that he was sitting here nervous and a little worried about the meeting. Sergi was sure that he wasn't going to let that happen again.

The only one at the table who wasn't nervous was Anton Turov. The Security Manager was quite happy with the whole situation. He could see the fear on the doctor's face and that fit right in with his plans. He watched Sergi out of his peripheral vision and knew the guy was feeling the heat. *Yes Sergi, you should be concerned.*

Turov had been given this position three months earlier, and had immediately started eying Sergi's job. All he saw was that the number-two was working closely with Alexi. That was his goal. He knew Alexi was terrifying. Everything about the guy radiated danger and complete control. This was who Turov wanted to learn from.

Turov had arrived with young Gusev, the other doctor. He knew this young doctor was as driven as he was, something about the doctor told him that he was as calculating and capable. This meeting couldn't start quickly enough. He was going to enjoy it.

The door opened and the huge figure looming in the hall stepped in. Alexi was a big man, even at his age. His shaggy gray hair hung loosely around his head. You were never sure where he was looking behind the dark glasses and hair hanging in his face. He walked slowly but deliberately to the head of the table. There were no canes, no limping, just an old body that was losing its strength.

The doctor and Sergi straightened in their chairs and stared down at the table. Turov turned and nodded to Alexi, unsure if he'd be acknowledged. Slowly Alexi lowered himself into the chair at the end on the table and opened up his laptop. He studied the screen for a long enough period of time to ensure his managers squirmed a bit.

Alexi didn't waste meetings going over numbers and listening to marketing plans. He got right to the point. "Doctor, what do you have for me this week?"

Zolkin cleared his throat, he knew this answer wouldn't be enough. "We haven't made any new ground Alexi. We still have limited numbers of subjects, and the lack of a clear objective makes it very hard to focus our efforts."

Alexi had heard it all before and was running out of patience. He had provided the doctor with plenty of subjects over the last three years. Dammit, did the man think subjects grew on trees? "Doctor I am starting to question if I have the right person for this project."

"I can assure you that I am well qualified to do this research. I have been trying my best, and I know I will get you to your goal."

Alexi blinked slowly. He had also heard that before and was starting to lose faith in the doctor.

"I understand that young Gusev is doing most of the work now. Correct?"

This was a tricky question, and the doctor took a second before answering, "I thought it was important to put him into the fire and let him get right at it. It seemed that since this is the main priority, he should focus on it."

Alexi wondered about that. His reports from security had seemed to imply that the doctor didn't have the heart for it, and was losing his passion for the project. He was starting to believe that Zolkin was giving young Gusev the work because he didn't want to do it himself. He needed to solve this because the project success depended on it. "Very well." He let the doctor stew for a while. "Sergi what about you? What do you have for me this week?"

"It was a crazy week sir. I didn't report on it last meeting because I didn't have all the facts, but we had a new prospect show up last week at the migraine support group." He stopped and took a breath. "Unfortunately, the crew lost both the subject and her companion. They may have been trained in martial arts, but either way, they managed to fight off the extraction crew and escape."

Alexi was both annoyed by the failure of his men and excited at the news of a new prospect. He wasn't patient either, "And that means what to me a week later?"

"Well Alexi, they came back this week and we made sure to have a better plan. Our crew had them in the van when those black guys and their crew ran our truck off the road and took them from us."

Alexi was livid. This was unacceptable.

"Two failures in two weeks." He just sat there and stared at Sergi. "Security tells me that the prospects were taken away in a truck. Did you follow?"

*****

What was this? Who had been out in the field from security? Sergi looked at Turov with narrowed eyes. The guy has been here a couple months and now he's watching Sergi's crews in the field. *Who the fuck did he think he was?* He locked eyes with Turov, sitting across the table, and caught the slight smirk on the man face. He realized he'd made a mistake downplaying the arrival of the new guy. This guy was a threat.

"My men couldn't follow sir, the van was demolished and beyond driving. It was towed back here."

"So your plan didn't include back-up? Or secondary plans for roadblocks, or other contingencies that arose?"

Sergi didn't answer. He looked down at his hands resting on the table. He had underestimated the targets, and then even when he knew there was a rogue group out there, he hadn't brought enough firepower or planning to the task. He wondered if the sweat from his palms would leave an imprint on the wood if he moved his hands.

"Alexi, I've asked to be allowed to get rid of these people that keep getting in our way. We know who most of them are and could easily round them up."

"Soldiers don't cry about logistics, or about civilians who get in their way. They go after their targets and succeed at all costs. That's what gives them pride. Don't you have any pride Sergi?"

Sergi was pissed now, he knew he should shut up, but couldn't resist one last question. "Did the security crew that was *following* my men find out where the woman was taken?"

Sergi saw Turov flinch before he managed to cover it with a smile.

"No, my man was told to just watch and not become involved. While he was watching your men lose the woman, someone sliced two of the tires on his car."

Alexi jumped into the conversation, "Sergi, don't be worrying about other departments. You clearly better get focused on your own problems, because you need to bring this woman in." He let the ramification of that sink in.

"What about this woman. What were her symptoms that triggered the extraction? Why is she important?"

"Our sitter at the meeting said she described a different aura and vision issue than the rest of the subjects." Sergi was happy that this was a question he could answer. "He said it wasn't even on the list we provided. It appears to be a new symptom."

*****

Alexi got excited every time there was a new angle or lead in the project. For the more than thirty years he had nurtured this idea, every time a new scrap of information came along it got him going. He'd wondered about the meaning of the message and where it could possibly have come from. And who put it there? It boggled his mind, and after all these years it still had him on the edge of his seat.

"Explain, Sergi."

"One of the criteria we have for the subjects is in the area of visual auras. After two years of research we understand the basic symptoms like blurry patches, or a hole in the visual field. We have lots of those here to study. We also know about flashes and extra stuff randomly overlaying the vision, and don't need more of those either."

"Our sitter at the Coney Island meeting said this woman had one clearly defined straight line that sometimes had crooks in it. This type of symptom isn't on our watch list because we've never seen it before."

This was good news. Alexi was sure this was an opportunity that they couldn't miss. The quicker they picked up the woman, the better. Would she be the one to break it all open? He wanted her now.

"What do we know about this couple?"

"We managed to grab their wallets with their address, but they haven't come home yet. The woman is Chantal Levi. A Canadian living in Manhattan. The guy is Gary Collins, American, same address."

"That's it Sergi?"

"We just got the wallets last night."

Alexi cut him off, "Give the wallets to Turov after the meeting." He turned to Turov, "I want everything on these two right away."

He looked around the table. These were the men he was depending on to complete his project. He planned to become very involved now that there was a potential breakthrough in the research.

"You men had better step up now. I want this. Do you understand?" Alexi stared at each of them in turn. "Now get out of here and bring me that woman." He pointed. "You doctor. Get me some results."

Two of the men scrambled to their feet, while the third got up slowly and followed them out of the room. These men were on thin ice, there would be no failure on this project. Not after all his time and sacrifice.

No, thought Alexi, no room for failure at all.

CHAPTER 13

Gary and Chantal made it through their second night. They spent Friday talking with others, and had resigned themselves to staying at least the weekend.

Now on Saturday morning Gary was eager to borrow a laptop again. He wanted to get back to searching for a way out of this mess. He had to put a plan in place – figure out their next steps.

Chantal was going to go out with some of the other woman and pick up some supplies. Gary had reminded her about medication and asked her to pick up lots of Tylenol and other pills for those that needed it. He wanted her to replace her bank cards and make sure she could get cash on the fly.

He knew he needed to get into his bank as well, and he also needed to fire off some client updates on the projects he had on the go. Again, these responsibilities went to the back burner as he dug into the computer. Right now the goal that was driving him was Septon Research.

On the surface the company wasn't any different than any other. Incorporated six years ago in New York City, after two years of construction, their facility came on line three years ago.

They claimed that their primary research was working with elderly patients to reduce memory loss. They had a great website explaining the effects of aging on the mind and the company's goals to make the lives of elderly people much better by increasing their mental capabilities.

A person would have thought it was a humanitarian organization. They should be nominated for a Nobel Prize in warm and fuzzy. He knew it was all a front. But it probably was enough to satisfy the cops every time they came sniffing around investigating claims of missing people. He could see why Dexter hadn't gotten anywhere.

He was sure they would have had clear records of people coming in and leaving after the studies. From Septon's point of view, there would be no missing people and none of the kidnapped would be showing up on any paper trail.

Anyone with some sense would ask why a company doing so much good would require such security. Gary was looking at photos of the place posted on the website. The pictures were obviously taken before the whole security structure was installed. The pictures showed a new building with nice green lawns fronting the street. Septon had obviously made sure to take the pictures before putting up fences and barbed wire. Anyone doing a web search would see this cozy looking company, and unless they went knocking on the door, wouldn't know the difference.

Deuces' photos showed razor wire and security cameras, which brought into question Septon's entire philosophy of using volunteers to help the world.

Gary moved on. Septon first showed up six years ago, there were no other facilities shown under that name. The problem was finding the faces behind the company.

The private company had no shareholders listed. Gary wasn't surprised that Septon was owned by a numbered company that was registered offshore. If this was as bad as he was starting to think, then he knew someone would have built an untraceable ladder to the top. If he did find a name it was probably going to be a well-paid front who turned out to be a clean, legit businessman.

Most companies splashed their executives all over the web these days. It was all about exposure and recognition. Septon wasn't faceless for no reason. He was sure of that. Fortunately, it wasn't a problem if you knew how to get to the bottom of it.

Everything was pointing to a crooked company. Criminals working behind a curtain. These types of things really got Gary pissed. There was no reason for it in today's world. with He believed that with hard work and a little luck everyone had a chance to reach some level of success. He really hated these criminal organizations. He'd seen a number of them in his life, but never personally in the U.S.. He couldn't sit still on this one.

His gut told him the danger to Chantal was real. It was obvious that these guys were serious enough about whatever they were doing to have tried to grab her. He'd been patient the last couple days while trying to get a handle on what was going on. What he was seeing was starting to piss him off.

He needed to change the flow of the situation. He had to act. He hated being reactive. He knew that they couldn't stay under Dexter's umbrella forever. Nor did he intend to.

Gary scrolled through his memory, revisiting the dictatorships, kingdoms and warlords he'd seen. He remembered coups, purges, and cleansings. He thought about what a cornered animal does when it feels it can't back up any more. It attacks, changing the field of battle and putting the attackers on the defensive.

Gary knew what he was thinking wasn't legal. But neither were Septon's actions. He was working along the rough edges of an idea, and the more he thought about it, the more he was sure it was the way to go. Getting Dexter on side would be the important part. He had no doubt about Deuce. That guy would be game.

Gary returned the laptop and went looking for Dexter. He was usually at the back where people could find him. If he wasn't there he was busy.

"Any news Dex?"

"News? We don't get much of that here. This place is settled in, we don't expect things to change much."

"You okay with that? I mean sitting down here and doing nothing?"

Dexter looked at Gary as if he didn't like his tone or the implications of his train of thought.

"You think I don't care, or what? That I'm scared?"

"No, I mean not being able to get to the bottom of this. To stop it dead."

Dexter softened a bit, "Well sure I want to stop it, but this is all I can do." He swung his arms around emphasising the shelter.

"What if I said I had a plan to change the playing field. Would you get behind it?"

Dexter's men didn't venture far over the next couple hours, concerned at the periodic shouting that broke out between the two men.

*****

Ivan peered over the operator's shoulder at the computer screen. This office building was another of his investments. On the top floor were a group of men with a bank of servers, computers, screens and cubicles.

You were well into Ivan's organization if you made it into this office. The details of his operation were laid out in these computers. They contained his contacts, contracts, and accounts – coded, filed, and ready for use. This team took care of computer security and financial systems. They knew how the bytes worked and how they could be manipulated.

"What do you mean you can't figure out who owns the numbered company?"

The young programmer didn't feel the sweat forming until a drop slid down his forehead. "Numbered companies off-shore are untraceable, always have been. We can tell you the country, and even the bank where it does business, but these guys are locked down tight. Offshore accounts work because those governments restrict outside access, have the best security programming, and deny access from outside by investigators."

"So give me the country and bank."

That question he could answer. "Antigua. Numbered company 12124561. They have two bank accounts in the American Commercial Credit Bank. From what we can see, it seems one is a company account and the other is personal."

"And you can't tell me how much cash is in there?"

"No sir. But I can tell you that money transfers into the U.S. and that none goes the other way. It's a one way deal."

Interesting. It meant that whoever was running the company had hidden a lot of cash away long before they started this company. Who owned the accounts and how much money was there?

"So what next?"

The young programmer felt the pressure starting to build again, "Well to have a bank account in Antigua you need to be a citizen or landowner. We are running a program trying to match names from their land registry with residents in the northeast U.S.. We have to hope that the man you want is here legally. If he is illegal then we can't track him."

That was what Ivan was afraid of. It was easy to live in the states without being legal. If you had money, you could do anything. Septon's crew was Russian, so it was safe to assume that the owner was too. This was unacceptable. No one should be doing business in his area without approval. The fact they had been operating entirely without his knowledge was an issue.

"You guys keep on it. I want to know who he is. Are we clear?"

All four men in the office answered in the affirmative, and Ivan was satisfied they understood his urgency. On the way back to the dojo he made a call on his cell. The long string of numbers would get him through to what was left of Russia, the area code was Kazakhstan.

Ivan issued new orders over the phone. The conversation went back and forth until he was finally sure expectations were clear. He leaned back in the truck and relaxed. Finally, he chuckled. He knew that running into Gary would lead to some interesting action. It always did.

Back in the dojo, he had Victor gather the men together. Ivan waited until all the men were paying attention before he started to tell them about the next day's mission. He wanted it clear what they were doing, why, and how important it was to him.

CHAPTER 14

Deuce had a different truck this time. Gary sat beside him waiting for the crew to get themselves set up out in the darkness. Gary was more and more impressed with Dexter. Trucks rotated on a weekly basis, sooner if they'd made contact with Septon. Last night they had talked for a long time while Dexter had explained everything he knew about Septon's soldiers.

They knew a lot. Over time they had narrowed down who worked where just by watching the facility from a distance. They knew who the doctors were, and who was cleaning staff. The soldiers had all been identified by watching who came and went from the garage.

Dexter said he figured there were about twelve soldiers who worked shifts. The research staff stayed at the facility around the clock. They didn't seem to leave. That was interesting. Were they there under their own will? Why keep them at the facility? The only reasonable reason was because you either didn't want them revealing what they are doing, or didn't want word getting out about what they are searching for.

That Dexter had someone watching the facility at all times clarified a few things. That was how they knew they were watching for a blue half-ton pickup truck tonight. One of their men was down at the exit to the industrial park, waiting to call when the half-ton was in sight. Gary was having a hard time being patient. Tonight he was going to hit them back.

The cell phone rang. The pickup was on its way. Gary could just make out the outlines of their crew standing in the shadows behind the building across the road. Deuce fired up the engine and put the transmission in gear. They watched the lights coming down the road. Timing would be everything.

Septon's soldier wouldn't think about the truck in the laneway. With the headlights off, the tinted windows would make the truck look empty and dark.

Deuce popped the clutch and the truck surged forward. He one-hopped it, switched gears and nailed it again. The truck slammed into the pickup just behind the front wheel and got enough of the door to push the vehicle sideways instead of spinning it. Deuce was getting pretty good at pushing vehicles off the road as he put the pickup onto the yard of the business across the street.

Deuce cranked the wheel and drove the pickup against a retaining wall in the parking lot. The pickup's driver slammed into the steering wheel when his vehicle hit the wall. The crew were on the truck before it stopped moving and as Deuce backed away from it, they ripped the man out of the pickup and dragged him to the back of the five-ton.

The doors quickly opened and arms reached down to grab the guy. He was pulled into the back of the truck and the rest of the crew climbed in. Someone banged a fist on the cab door, signalling that they were in. Deuce slammed the truck into gear and they roared out of the industrial park.

They weren't going back to the warehouse. Dexter had been clear about that. No trouble for the underground. Deuce drove to the west side of Brooklyn. Turning off into one of the housing projects, he pulled into a parking lot in a rundown area.

Gary had suggested that they come to this kind of spot. Deuce pulled the truck to the far end of the lot and backed up against a rusted fence. He turned to Gary, "How long you need?"

"Just have your men spread out, and stay close to the truck. Keep a couple in the cab ready to go. You and me will be in the back. I'm not sure how long it will take."

It was dark out and Gary looked up, knowing he couldn't see anyone, but was sure there were people looking down from the apartments, checking out the truck.

They climbed in the back and slid the door closed. In the dim light Gary murmured a few directions and moved forward in the compartment. Deuce threw the switch that flooded the truck with light.

The man on the floor must have been scared, Gary could see the panic on his face. He'd been in the dark since being grabbed and hadn't moved from where he'd been thrown on the floor. Now Gary watched him scramble to put his back against the wall, while he looked around the compartment. Then he looked at Gary's face.

He knew he had the guy's attention. The flicker of recognition in the Septon soldier's eyes meant he must have been one of the men trying to kidnap Chantal. Gary shook his head slowly and spoke in clear Russian, "Doesn't look good my friend. You recognise a bad situation?"

The guy would be trying to figure out things, to see if he had an angle out of this mess. Gary watched him look around the compartment again, this time a little more focused. When he saw Deuce his eyes snapped open. He wasn't happy seeing the massive black man standing quietly in the corner.

"Ah, you've seen my friend. Good. I don't think he's your friend though, which as you can imagine is not so good." He let that settle while the guy took another quick look back at Deuce.

"What have I done to you or this man? I am no one. I don't know you… Please."

"Bullshit. You work for Septon. Are you telling me that you think what you do there is okay?"

"No, it's not okay. But I have a family to take care of and these guys pay really good. You don't know how it is, you just don't quit these guys. They brought me and my family from Belarus. You can understand now why I need to walk carefully and stay loyal."

Gary could see his conflict. Some of these guys were hard-core criminals, killing was like breathing for them. It was just a part of life. Others were in it for the money and didn't want to do anything too gruesome or incriminating. Gary could tell this guy was one of the second type. This would make it easier.

If this one had been hard core it would have been hard to make him talk. Unless he was going to torture the guy – which was something he'd seen, but never done himself – the threat of Deuce pounding him wouldn't have worked. The tough guy would just take the beating. Only torture would work on those guys. This guy however might be easier.

"I need you to answer some questions for me. Or you have the choice of meeting my friend." He waved his arm back towards Deuce. "His sister was taken by Septon years ago. He's had time to imagine his revenge."

Hoping the guy really was in over his head and had a family and people to go home to, Gary started.

"Why do you take the people?" He was relieved to see the guy sit up straight and prepare to answer.

"Someone in the office decides who gets taken and they call us out to snatch them off the street and bring them back to the facility."

"Why?"

"I don't know. Some type of research. We never see where the people are taken inside the building. We are kept in the back, on call at the garage. I don't think it's good."

"Why do you say that?"

"Some of the men who have been there longer than me say that they've heard screaming sometimes when they have been inside the building."

Gary had known it was a chance taking a soldier. His captive might have limited information, but he'd also been the easiest to get. He had to agree that screaming in a research facility didn't sound like a good thing.

He had the feeling he wasn't going to get much more here. He got the man to name his other co-workers and crew leader. "Who does your boss report to?"

"A fucking lunatic. Russian guy named Sergi."

Intriguing. "Why is he a lunatic?"

"When we missed you the first week and then lost you the second, Sergi shot the old crew leader in the head in front of everyone in the garage." The guy shivered at the memory.

Gary figured they'd gotten as much as he could from the soldier. The question was what to do with him. There were a number of possibilities. Now he had to choose one. He didn't want to hurt him, but he didn't want him alerting Septon either.

That they would have to sit on him, it had been one of the options they'd already discussed. Deuce had somewhere he could be kept. The guy would get out of it alive and well, if he could suffer being held hostage for a while. Surely a punishment which fit the crime.

They loaded the crew back into the five-ton and Deuce drove them across town to another group of low-rental housing units.

They dropped off the guy with some friends of Deuce's who weren't too happy. They didn't mind keeping him, they just didn't like the rule about treating him okay. Gary let the big guy work that one out with his buddies and just hoped the hostage made it through to the end in one piece.

Finally headed home, Gary was able to relax and let the adrenaline seep out of his body. Now he was positive Septon was taking people, for the first time he thought of it as experimenting on them instead of doing research. Experimenting fit the screaming scenario better.

Gary's eyes stayed closed until Deuce broke the silence, "You better have a plan man, because I really wanted to do that Russian harm. We could have really hurt him."

"Easy Deuce. Let me get to the bottom of things and then we can do some real damage."

"Yeah, well that fuck is safe for now, but one phone call and he ain't safe no more."

Gary understood, and let it go. He wanted to solve this puzzle as much as they did. These types of things ate at him and he knew he wouldn't let Deuce down. He was relieved when they bounced over the curb at the back of the warehouse. They'd made it back in one piece.

CHAPTER 15

Sunday morning was perfect for Ivan's plan. His men were in place while he sat in a second truck parked down the street to watch the proceedings. One of his men had been watching the place since they had been given Septon's name.

His phone rang, and Ivan answered it impatiently. "What?"

"It's me. I have some news." Ivan waited for Gary to continue, "We decided to turn the tables, and grabbed one of their soldiers. I couldn't torture the guy, but he gave us everything he had. Listen, they are taking people and I think it's bad. Like they're doing experimentation instead of research."

Ivan didn't see much difference between the two, but kept that to himself. "Okay, I'll get back to you." He hung up and went back to his operation. He wasn't surprised that Gary had gone on the offensive, just that he'd beaten him to it. Well, he wasn't going after a soldier with limited access, and he sure didn't have a problem with torture. He had the marks to prove he'd learnt well.

If you end up in prison in the wrong country, it never was the beatings that got to you. After too many of those, you didn't even flinch when you were kicked. There was a numbness that took over.

What got to you were the psychological attacks from things like light depravation, or noise bombardment, and being forced into painful positions and held that way for days. The constant screams of others enduring their interrogations were as bad as enduring your own. That Gary had been the one to pull him out of one of those places was just another tie in the journey they were on.

Ivan chuckled at thought of Gary in the thick of things again, then quickly snapped back to the present on full alert. His men were moving. The shift had ended and the cleaning staff were being replaced.

The old man drove a small car through Septon's gates. He would be stopping at the traffic-activated light at the end of the industrial park. One of those ones that stayed red until an approaching car triggered the sensor embedded in the asphalt.

The man standing on the sidewalk looked like he was going to cross when the light changed. Instead he took four or five quick steps towards the car, pulling out a small sledgehammer. As he took the last step he raised the hammer, bringing it down towards the car.

The old man didn't have time to think. The hammer smashed through the window. When he looked out the opening, he was met by a pair of hands reaching in for him. He tried to scramble towards the passenger seat but the hands had him by the collar.

Ivan watched his man smash the window and pull the man clear of the car. An SUV pulled up beside the car as the man was dragged out of the car window, towards the back of the rig. Two men lifted him and dropped him in the back, climbing in behind him. Ivan's man calmly walked back to the car and retrieved his hammer.

Ivan sat for about fifteen minutes after the SUV drove away and watched for the sight of police showing up or anything out of the ordinary. Finally it was time to talk to the old man. He nodded to Victor.

"Let's go."

His men were waiting in the back of a shipping company he owned, which was empty at night except for security. Ivan didn't mind this part of the job. Having power and money were his goals, but every once in a while you had to get dirty. It came with the territory.

The old man tied to a chair in the middle of a closed shipping dock looked in relatively good shape. Ivan's men hadn't touched him yet. He walked up and had a good look at the man's face. It would sometimes tell him a lot. The way the old man was staring back told Ivan he had some backbone.

He was willing to bet that the old man had been in the thick of it at some time in his life. You could see in his eyes that he wasn't scared. Defiance. Ivan had to be careful. Old men could be hard to interrogate. They knew they were getting close to the end, having been tough all their lives, they could decide that this age wasn't the time to roll over.

Ivan stood there and stared back at the old man, "So you going to tell me what I want to know old man?"

The prisoner never wavered his gaze, just spit. Ivan jumped back and laughed. "Okay old man, have it your way." The man was tough and loyal to his boss, it could be for a number of reasons. Indebted to the boss, the boss could have something over him, could be a relative. He stepped back to talk to his right hand Victor in a quiet tone, "Where's his wallet?"

"I have it."

"Get on the phone, run his name and get me an address."

Ivan turned back to the old man. If he was going to get anything at all from this guy, he would need leverage. While he waited for that he would have to loosen him up. It was the only way he'd believe the threat. He slipped off his jacket and started rolling up his sleeves.

He yelled to no one in particular, "Get me a bucket of ice." He'd kept his eyes on the man. Ivan saw the slight flicker in his captive's eyes that said he knew what the ice was for. This was interesting. The man had seen people tortured before.

"So you understand the process. Good. You know I need to shake you up a little first." Ivan stepped closer and drove his fist into the man's face. The chair flew backwards and the man landed hard on the floor. Two men ran forward and lifted the chair back to its upright position.

The difference was immediate. The man's face was covered in blood running from his smashed-in nose, past his mouth, dripping off his chin. The old man's eyes hadn't changed though, he kept his stare locked onto Ivan.

He stepped forward and hit him again. This time there was a grunt from the old man. Ivan was impressed, he'd expected a scream. The shot right in the same spot, punishing already broken bones, should have hurt like hell. Either way, the chair went over backwards again.

When the chair was upright, the old man's eyes were blurry as he choked a bit on the blood in his mouth. Ivan watched as the old man got himself under control.

Ivan wanted the old man feeling on top of things. Feeling that all he had to do was hold out long enough and he would win this thing. The old man would know that it might end in his death, but he'd made that call already. Since the old man thought he knew where this was going, Ivan would accommodate him.

"Okay old man, you must also know that eventually I'll get serious." Ivan again kept his gaze on his captive as he called out to anyone in his crew, "Industrial pliers." When someone put a pair in his hand, he swung them back and forth to get used to the weight. They were nice and heavy.

The old man was trying hard not to squirm, but Ivan knew the old man had to know somewhere in his head that this thing could do real damage. If it was him, he'd be calculating the weight and trying to push aside the images his brain would be conjuring of what was going to happen next.

"Do you want to answer some questions before we proceed?" Ivan continued to wave the pliers in a slow arc, back and forth. The old guy didn't spit this time, but he did force a smile onto his swollen face. That was what Ivan had expected and he swung the pliers a little higher on the next pass.

As his arm came back, Ivan put his weight into it and drove the pliers down into the guy's knee. There was an audible crack, and a scream, as the steel broke the old bone into fragments. He had known the guy wouldn't be able to hold that one in. Breaking bones can be really painful.

"Oh, come now old man, we're just getting started," he was about to continue when he heard a phone ringing. He watched

Victor take a call before turning back. He didn't give him much recovery time. Instead he reached forward grabbing the man's head with one hand and then came in with the pliers and caught his bottom lip.

He felt the man stiffen, so he knew the guy was with him on this one. He squeezed the handles and felt the lip flatten at the same time he twisted up and away. There was a moment when everything went tight and the pliers were either going to slide off the lip or rip it away. Ivan twisted and squeezed more, and finally felt the skin ripping loose, as a piece of lip tore free. He held the pliers up for the old man to see, but his victim's eyes were closed tight and his face was twisted in pain.

Ivan heard a few of his own men shifting their weight around, clearing their throats at the sight of the hanging skin. Ivan threw the pliers on the ground. He listened to Victor for a moment as his lieutenant whispered into his ear. Smiling at the news, Ivan pulled a chair forward so he could sit nice and close.

"Well old man, it's time we get serious. I needed you to understand that I am capable of doing the dirty work, and that it doesn't bother me. You understand?"

Ivan watched concern replace courage on the old man's face. He still wouldn't talk, he was sure of that now, at least not without leverage. He was clearly a tough old bastard, and ready to die for some misguided sense of loyalty. Well, that was fine with him, he wanted to give the man a second chance to decide where his loyalty really lay.

"I hope old man that you didn't make the mistake of thinking you were my target." He watched the old man trying to focus.

"No, you are too stubborn and too hard. There are much easier people I can get to answer questions. There are people out there who are not as hard as you. People who live here in New York. Like the people at 18th street and 22nd avenue."

Ivan waited for the old man to realize that was his neighbourhood, and to come to the understanding that the man sitting in front of him knew where his wife and daughter lived. The old man's whole demeanour changed as all the strength drained out of him, and Ivan knew he was ready to answer questions.

"So maybe you understand now old man. Now, I want to know what is going on in this facility." Ivan bent down to make sure he was looking right into the old man's eyes. "And lie to me just once and these people you care for are gone forever."

The man coughed again and tried to speak, "They do experiments on the people. I don't see them. I only clean up at nights when no one is there." He stopped for a moment, "It's very bad there. I clean up blood and stuff some nights. The daytime cleaner says they hurt people in that place. No one ever goes home."

"How many people in there?"

"Many people. There are cells to keep them. They bring them out for the experiments and use them until they are no good to anyone. The bodies are taken to an incinerator somewhere in the city. I know, because once a week I load them onto the truck in the middle of the night."

Ivan was fuming, he could rip the guy's head off right now, but needed the information. He was really taking a disliking to this Septon Research and couldn't believe they were getting away with this stuff. "What are the experiments about?"

"The day-time cleaner said he saw the doctors trying to make these people have headaches. They were doing horrible things to the people while the doctors would be shouting and asking what they saw." He stopped again because his breathing had sped up. "When the people don't tell the doctors what they want, they increase the torture, like they are trying to force the people to see something. It makes no sense."

No it didn't. At least not to Ivan. He knew this stuff was important, but not why.

Ivan asked questions about the doctors and other employees. He wanted descriptions of all the staff, especially those who seemed like bosses. The one who was the most intriguing was an older man with greying hair who was hardly ever seen, but seemed to have everyone's respect whenever he was around. The old man had indicated that he thought this might be the boss.

Ivan sat back for a while and thought about what to do with the old man. He sure wasn't going back to Septon. Ivan got up and walked away. He stopped beside Victor. "Take this man and his family, I want them put on one of our ships going home. He doesn't deserve to be here."

Ivan used the water in the bucket of ice to clean his hands and rolled down his sleeves while Victor issued instructions to the other men. He kicked the bucket over to the old man and indicated to Victor it was time to go.

He wanted to think about this whole thing some more, but knew Gary would want whatever information he had come up with. He pulled out his cell.

CHAPTER 16

When Sergi got into work on Monday morning he was a little uneasy at the sight of a red-flagged email announcing an emergency meeting first thing.

He placed a quick call to security, but the man there either didn't have anything to offer, or had been instructed not to talk to him. He had a bad feeling about this, but didn't know why. Either way, he couldn't avoid the meeting, and headed down the hall.

Sergi got another bad feeling when he entered the room where Alexi and Turov were already seated at the far end of the table. The two of them stopped talking as he arrived. The three men waited in silence until Sergi casually asked, "Where is the damned doctor? We usually don't have to wait for him."

"Don't worry about the doctor." There was a hint of displeasure in Alexi's voice, "Bring us up to date on these latest events, tell me how you plan to react."

Sergi was confused, he didn't know about any new events and quickly realized he had been deliberately left in the dark. "Excuse me sir, what events are you questioning?"

"Are you not aware of what is happening around here Sergi? As my number-two you must know that we are under attack"

"What do you mean, sir?"

"Tell him, Turov."

The security manager took the lead with half a smirk on his face and a scolding tone in his voice, "One of your men was kidnapped on the way into the industrial park on Saturday evening. His truck was found by my security in the middle of the night." Turov let Sergi absorb the news long enough to realize he was out of touch.

"One of our cleaners was also grabbed as he left the facility Sunday morning. His car was found stopped at the lights, with the driver's window smashed in.

The room was quiet while Alexi asked, "So Sergi, do you know what's going on here?"

"No. No, I don't know, but I'll get on it right away."

"What do you think, Turov? Do you think Sergi is up to the task?" Their boss raised an eyebrow.

What the fuck? Sergi only answered to Alexi, what the hell did Turov have to do with it?

The contempt was evident in the young security manager's voice. "No I don't. I think Sergi is behind events, instead of in front of them. And I don't see any reason this would change. I don't think he has any devotion to the cause. He may be just enjoying the ride. He might be getting complacent."

Unfortunately for Sergi, Alexi was wondering the same thing. In fact he was sure of it. Sometimes change was needed. "Anything else, Turov?"

"Yes sir, there is. I also wonder if the reason Sergi isn't successful is because he shares too much compassion for the subjects. Perhaps the fact he also suffers these headaches clouds his drive."

Sergi bumped his knee against the underside of the table as he jumped in his chair. *What?* "Excuse me?"

"We have cameras everywhere in this facility, even your office. I can bring in the video of you rubbing your head and squeezing your temples, if you need me to."

Alexi was intrigued now. He hadn't known this, it had been a question he'd asked Sergi back at the beginning. So Sergi had lied. Well that would be his problem now. "This is bad news for you if it is true. Tell me that it is not," he said quietly.

Sergi knew he was in trouble now. He needed to try and get out of this in one piece. "Alexi, it is only in the last year that I have had some minor tension headaches. They are nothing to worry about, definitely not migraines. And I assure you I am totally committed to the project."

Alexi turned to nod at Turov who quickly picked up a cell phone and started dialling. Alexi turned back to Sergi, "I'm grateful you are still committed to us Sergi. I am going to give you an opportunity to help us."

Sergi was quick to respond, "Thank you Alexi, I will show you."

The door opened, and four men Sergi had never seen before came into the room. He looked at Alexi in confusion. Alexi brushed the hair slightly from his face. He wanted Sergi to see his smile. "I am going to send you down to the experimentation section of the facility and we will see if the doctors can use your help."

Sergi started to feel claustrophobic, he could feel a dampness spreading down the center of his spine. "What do you mean, I could help them?" He knew what went on over there.

"They will like a new subject who is just starting to get headaches. I'm sure they'll want to see you immediately."

The scream was piercing. It took Sergi a second to realise it was his own. He jumped up as the waiting men swarmed him and quickly had him under control. As they dragged him out the door, he called over his shoulder, "Alexi. Alexi, please."

The two men in the meeting room listened to the screaming fading down the hall. Alexi stated simply, "You are the number-two now. Don't disappoint me."

"No, sir!" The new man of authority kept a calm exterior, but inside he was grinning with delight.

Alexi got up and walked to the door, his last words to Turov were clear, "You need to change the attitude around here. I want that girl. Now."

"Yes, Sir!"

Turov headed back to his office. He had a lot to do. He would have to ensure the soldiers were really up to the task. He'd need replacements, plus he wanted to double the total number of men.

He needed to set up surveillance on the men in Sergi's files who had been giving Septon trouble over the years. They were obviously stepping up their game. Turov wanted the fuckers gone, and he wouldn't be waiting to ask the boss for approval. He would do whatever it took to succeed. There were a number of things to get to and he had no time to waste.

CHAPTER 17

Gary walked around aimlessly. It was Monday morning and he had to decide what to do. The idea of going home today was out of the question. Ivan's phone call had been disturbing to say the least.

That Ivan had grabbed someone to squeeze for information wasn't really a surprise. The information he acquired was. Gary had assumed this whole thing was something to do with medical research about migraines, but this was something altogether different.

Ivan told him that Septon was forcing the people to have migraines and then torturing them to get some kind of information out of them. They were being asked what they saw. *What?* What were they looking for or hoping to find? What could a bunch of people suffering in the middle of a migraine do for Septon? He had so many questions, but didn't know where to start.

Ivan's last words had left Gary speechless, "Whatever Septon is doing, there are people dying, because they take a load of bodies to an incinerator every week."

When Gary finally did reply, he was a little shaky, "Fuck me, Ivan, this is crazy." They'd agreed on that, and decided they were going to try and figure out who Septon's owner was. When he hung up he knew he hadn't really been truthful. He was going to stay on the problem, but he kept returning to whatever it was that Septon was looking for.

It seemed to him that Septon thought something was supposed to happen to people when they had migraines. Ivan's comment about the captives being asked what they were seeing, led him to the conclusion this had something to do with the twenty percent of sufferers who had visual auras.

Chantal had described hers at that first meeting. The soldier that he and Deuce had picked up said she had new symptoms that weren't listed in their criteria. Was it the aura she described? Having that thought, Gary decided to go see where she was.

She was writing in a notebook when Gary sat down beside her to fill her in. He took the time to explain what he and Ivan had been up to. She was pissed that Gary had gone out without telling her, but the new intel on Septon seemed to shake her the most.

"I really don't think we're going home right now. Now that I know what they're doing, maybe I can try to figure out why, and then shut them down."

"Down here?"

"Think about it," he responded. "I have a bunch of people with migraines right here to work with. I couldn't ask for better."

Chantal couldn't argue with that. Gary did have a point there. She really wanted to get out of this place, but had become more involved with the people herself over the last couple of days. "I figured you would want to stay."

She opened the book up again, "I was working on a list of things these people need."

Gary was relieved. It would have been hard if she'd wanted to leave. He wouldn't have been able to let her, which could have been more than a little difficult.

Dexter and a group of men were building another set of sleeping quarters out of two-by-fours, curtained off with canvas. Gary caught Dexter's eye, and motioned to an empty table. The two men sat down.

He knew it was hard on Dexter when he told him about the bodies being taken to incinerators. If Dexter had held out any hope his father might be alive inside Septon, it was slipping now. The big guy was as confused as everyone else about why Septon would want information from the headaches.

Gary got to the point, "I have an idea, but I need your support, because we'd need the help of the people here."

"What do you want to do?" Dexter was watching him closely.

"I want to do my own research. I want to talk to the people here and see if we can figure out what Septon is after."

Dexter couldn't see a problem. In the back of his head he knew it was a worth the try, and besides, the people in here could use something to focus on. "So what do you want from me?"

"Get everyone together at the tables in the back at noon hour. I'll talk to them and take it from there."

*****

Gary wasn't surprised when he and Chantal arrived at the meeting area and found pretty much the whole group already there. He knew everyone wanted out of there, and any solution was worth working on. He caught Dexter's eye and nodded, then turned to the group. Where to begin?

He introduced himself and shared his and Chantal's story. He explained that he wanted to do something about the whole mess they were all in.

Carefully he laid out the new intelligence they had gathered, explaining he was pretty sure that Septon was looking only at those migraines with auras. Gary wanted people with auras to move to one side. Slowly, they separated from family or friends, and moved for him. Chantal walked over and put herself with the new group.

The fifteen were mostly adults with a couple of teenagers mixed in. Gary didn't know where he was going, but it was time to start.

"It seems that you are important in this and I need your help. I think the best way to start is by breaking into groups sorted by what type of images you see during a headache. So anyone who is missing parts of their vision, like holes or blank spots, move over here." Gary pointed to the left. "Those of you that have something extra added to your vision, like lines or dots, move over to the right."

He wanted to know the extent of their problems. He started with the group that had spot blindness, where a part of their vision was missing. But they all described different scenarios. One of them said his spots could cover up to a quarter of his sight, which was a big spot. He'd have to keep moving his head left and right to make sure he could see what was hidden by the spot. Another said he would get six or seven little blind spots that would move around in his vision like in a kaleidoscope. He would have a hard time focusing on what was in front of him because he kept getting distracted following the moving dots.

Two other people described complete loss of vision on one side. Both eyes were working, and as the person looked straight ahead she would see everything from center all the way around to the one side, and nothing on the other. She couldn't see much past the halfway point and had to constantly swivel from side to side to see.

He decided to separate the spot auras from the half vision auras. Next he turned to the rest of the group who had things added to their vision. Gary wanted to get an idea what they were seeing and how it looked when it was mixed with the regular vision.

Gary noticed a hesitancy from this group initially. He realized it was easier to admit you were having a blind spot and something missing from your vision than it was to admit you were seeing things. The first guy was quick to point out that he pretty much always saw the same thing. Just a long bar that ran up and down in the middle of his vision. Same result as the blind spot, you needed to move your head constantly to try and see around it.

The next person said that everything was out of shape. Buildings would have odd shapes or things sticking out of them and be out of square. Not everything was misshapen, but the things that were made walking around seem like a house of mirrors.

Some of the conditions didn't seem as bad as others. The one woman said she saw little dots in perfect rows covering her whole visual area, but she could almost ignore them and look right through. Gary came to the conclusion that he could break these symptoms in to two groups as well.

The first group would be those with additions, like a bar or dots, that were always in the same place and the second would be those whose additions to their visions were random and could show up anywhere.

Okay, he had split them into four groups. Now what? He didn't know. He had them here and they were willing, but was he supposed to do to them? What was he looking for?

"Okay, this is what I'm thinking. I'd like to talk to you one-on-one and understand your headaches. However, if anyone has symptoms or feels a headache coming on over the next day please come to me and let me ask questions. This is really important."

Gary was thinking that he needed to watch the people have their auras. He definitely wanted to be there when they happened. He couldn't force them like Septon, but hopefully the people would come to him.

He made arrangements to visit with each of them over the next few hours and took a bunch of notes on their individual stories. He needed as much information as he could gather. He was still confused as hell. None of this stuff was pointing to a solution.

"You know, compared to some of these people, I've got it pretty good." Chantal pushed her dinner plate to the side. "Hello in there." She waved her hand in front of Gary's face.

"Yeah, yeah. Sorry. Just trying to wrap my brain around all this."

"You can do this," she smiled. "You're a fixer. You just get stuff done. I've watched you invent some amazing solutions in your work that nobody else could even think of."

"I don't know. This whole thing makes no sense." He shook his head.

"Look what you did for that mine in Brazil."

"That project's not done yet."

"As soon as that German understands how much better his mine runs, the whole project will come out perfect."

Gary laughed. "Since he's refused to negotiate with the strikers, he might not be too happy when he discovers that I plan to give them productivity bonuses out of my share."

"But the strike will be over."

"That's the plan."

"See. I told you. You think differently. It's brilliant."

Gary smiled. He hoped so. He was going to need everything he had to figure out this Septon problem.

He still had questions. What was he supposed to do with these auras? What were they supposed to do? He had to step back a bit, he felt too close to the problem. He needed to look at it as a whole. Why manipulate someone with a headache? It could only be for so many reasons. Either they had some sort of knowledge that you wanted out of them, or you wanted them to do something for you.

Was there something related between migraine suffers? How would you figure it out? There had to be something to gain from doing this, or else why do it? Septon was spending a lot of money and taking a lot of risk.

He was sure there was something here, but not sure what. "I'm thinking about too much. There has to be a reason to this. There has to be a message or information or something…" his voice trailed off.

Did the visual defects have a purpose? He still needed more, but what? He turned to Chantal, "Septon seemed pretty interested in your aura. They said it was different from the others. Tell me more about it."

"It's just a line that appears and stays there in the front of my eye until the meds start to work. I guess since it's been there for years, I've gotten used to it."

"Was it always the same line, even back in the beginning?"

"Pretty much. It's always been a black line. The direction the line takes has changed over the years, but not the size."

"Does the direction of the line change a lot? "

"No, not really, it's been the same for the last four or five years."

Again he wasn't sure where to go, but the word *directions* kept slipping into his head. He wondered about the effects migraines had on Chantal, "It doesn't bother you having this line in your vision every time you have a migraine?" Gary thought it would drive him nuts.

"Actually no, not any more. When you get the migraine you're worrying more about the pain you know is coming than anything else. Vision issues are secondary, after all, they don't hurt. I never pay it much attention anymore."

"Is the line like something?" Gary asked. "What does it remind you of?"

She thought about his question for a moment, "It's funny really, because it reminds me one on those GPS map things you can get in your car for directions. Sometimes my eyes trace the line like following a map."

Somewhere tumblers were tripping in his brain. Something Chantal had just said was turning things over. Could Septon be after directions to somewhere?

If so, that would mean the auras were embedded. If they were embedded in the brain, then they must have a purpose. He knew it was a huge leap, but he had nothing else.

Gary got up and started to pace. Ten strides from the tables to the kitchen. Fourteen strides to the sleeping area. The more he thought about it, the more he liked it. He'd been thinking that it was about a message. But he'd had a problem with that. His problem was the absence of words. Messages usually revolved around words and no one was mentioning words or speaking.

What these people were describing were visions and objects, lines and dots. Ivan said Septon's doctors asked what the people saw when they were under the migraines.

Twelve steps back to the table. Gary frowned as he thought about objects and lines. Were the auras pointing towards directions and not a message? If so, directions to where?

CHAPTER 18

Alexi was impressed with the tour to this point. Seeing the changes Turov had put in place when he replaced Sergi only made him angry with himself for having let things slip over time.

The garage area had a group of men engaged in hand-to-hand combat training, while others tore down and cleaned their guns. Looking around he counted twenty. Turov explained that others were out on patrol and that effective immediately, anyone entering the industrial park was under surveillance.

Alexi liked this enthusiasm. It was the way he liked to operate, calmly, quietly and in complete control, but with a fire driving from within. Turov was showing him that he too was committed to success, and would do whatever was required to complete the project. He knew how to use men with drive. He'd been doing it all his life.

Turov led the way as they headed for the research wing of the facility. A security guard buzzed them through, and they headed directly to the doctor's offices.

Alexi didn't expect anyone to be there. The doctors should be with the subjects in the experimental labs. However, Turov was certain he would find something else. Sure enough, when the two men entered the offices, there was Doctor Zolkin sitting at this desk, shuffling through a stack of paper.

Turov stepped aside as Zolkin literally jumped up from his chair at the sudden appearance of his boss. He looked down at the papers strewn across his desk, it looked like he'd been there for hours. Every one of the files that were spread out over the desk was open.

Alexi was angry. He didn't pay this man to sit in his office, especially after he'd been told to get better results.

"Zolkin, you can't possibly be getting me the results you promised if you're holed up in your office. What are you doing?"

The doctor had no answer. He was hiding, pure and simple. Sergi being brought down to the research wing had sent him over the edge. Now they wanted him experimenting on their own staff. Who was next? He looked at the folders that were spread across his desk.

"I am updating our files with the latest results and preparing a test schedule for," he stalled, "for Sergi."

"How do you expect to find a solution sitting in your office doctor?" Alexi's voice had taken on accusatory tone.

"I have Gusev running experiments as we speak. Everything is going as planned."

"Really doctor. Why don't we go and see this work that's being done. Show me what you are doing."

The doctor's legs wobbled a little as he held onto the table for a moment. Finally, he led them out the door and down the hallway towards the labs.

Alexi was becoming desperate to get to the end of this journey. He had come a long way, and yet so close to the end, he still couldn't reach his goal. He was a patient man and had learned his lessons well. Recruited right from university, he'd had to choose between the GRU and the KGB, because they took all the top students.

It had been okay for him, he had expected big things from himself. The thought of a clerical job, or worse, a civilian position, had been revolting. He was destined, that was how he'd looked at it. The GRU fielded agents in foreign countries and as a proud Russian Alexi decided to stay at home and joined the Committee for State Security, known as the KGB.

A military branch, under military law and leadership, the KGB was responsible for internal security, intelligence, and the secret police. He had believed back then that the Soviet Union was the strongest country in the world and that they were within their rights to try to control as much of the planet as they could.

That was how he ended up in Cuba at the age of twenty as a paper-pusher doing administrative support at the height of the Cuban Missile Crisis. Cuba was where Alexi had found his calling. It was where he witnessed his first torture sessions and became completely enthralled with bending others to his will.

At that time everything was going to hell and the whole plan was falling apart. At his age the politics and international dynamics were outside his understanding, but his team were interrogating Cubans to see if there had been leaks, trying to find out who was helping the Americans.

Alexi had been able to watch a number of sessions where he had been called in to record events. He watched as a skilled interrogator had calmly scared the hell out of people, forcing them to provide answers. He had been fascinated with the control the interrogator had, and the amount of pain and terror he could cause. He had been sure he could do the same thing.

After he was accepted into the interrogation services, he practiced his skills on local criminals and political activists in Russian until the Vietnam War started. When the Russians decided to back the North Vietnamese, Alexi was able to really hone his skills in the jungles of Southeast Asia.

He didn't put any value on life, he just didn't care. When he had a subject to work on he was focused only on the results and had the ability to shake it off afterwards. Alexi had been alone with prisoners of war on so many occasions that by the end he was experimenting with new methods. When one subject died he never skipped a beat, starting in on the next one.

He'd always known when there was no information left to get from a subject, but he would continue to push buttons and try different techniques to get more effective reactions. It was during one of those late night sessions, that it happened for the first time. Something was said that he could personally capitalize on.

The man had told Alexi that his family had buried everything they had to avoid losing it during the war. He had jumped all over the captive and then made a deal with a few North Vietnamese to find it and dig it up. Alexi had never thought of personal gain before, but as he left Vietnam he was now a seasoned killer who enjoyed the work and looked for ways to capitalize on it.

In '79, when the war began in Afghanistan, he was in his prime. At thirty-four years old he was a senior interrogator working in support of the fighting forces. There was a steady stream of prisoners brought in to be questioned.

Over the next ten years Alexi and his team would torture and interrogate hundreds of Mujahedeen and villagers in the small building they occupied on the main base. He dug into their victim's personal lives, seeking more than just the standard military information. The team of senior interrogators all did well as a group, sharing in any cash or treasures the interrogations turned up.

The war went badly for the Soviet Union. As badly as the American experience did in Vietnam. A guerrilla war was unwinnable unless you were going to move in with millions of soldiers and take over the country and occupy it. But for the interrogators it was quite profitable.

This was where Alexi had first learned about the headaches and some sort of message. A group had been brought in that had been captured along the border, they had seemed to be trying to leave Afghanistan. The person Alexi was working on had eventually confessed that the group was following a message that they all had received because of bad headaches. He kept insisting they were going to a new world.

Alexi had been floored, what headaches and what message? He had spent late nights with each of the group and they all said the same thing. No one could tell him what the message was, or what was really happening, because they all said that the person who was leading them had disappeared, that he wasn't part of the group that had been captured. Alexi knew then that he was onto something.

He had troops looking everywhere in the same area that the group was picked up in hopes of finding this leader, but had never been able to turn him up. The other interrogators wanted to know why he was so preoccupied with this particular group of captives, and he would shake them off. He knew a few of the others were getting suspicious, afraid that he was holding back on some sort of lucrative information, but he kept quiet and kept working the group.

The most interesting thing Alexi came away with was that the people in the group didn't care about the war, or their fellow countrymen. They had been on some kind of mission driven by something they saw when they were suffering headaches. Alexi had never gotten any further, and eventually, due to his interrogation techniques, he had no subjects left.

Alexi and the team returned to Russia after the war ended and went on to extract information from Russian locals about their hidden secrets and treasures. The team had a number of long-term caches waiting to be recovered, but they were patient.

He quietly left the country immediately after the fall of communism and the breakup of the Soviet Union. The KGB was disbanded and he disappeared. He hadn't wanted to be on the receiving end of any retaliation, or revenge rampages, by the locals. He had made a lot of enemies in his home country.

He'd bounced around a bit before ending up in the U.S. in the late '90s. He'd chosen the Brighton Beach area of New York because of its large Russian population. It took him a few years to gather up and retrieve all the money he had hidden away. Finally, he set up Septon and got back to work on his research.

Alexi felt frustrated as he walked down the hall. He had thought it would be so easy once he had a facility with the right people working on the problem. Now there was this new woman with different symptoms than he had ever seen before, and he wanted her in here. He wanted to experiment on her himself.

The three men entered the first laboratory. A quick look around told them Gusev wasn't there. Zolkin explained that the subjects in this lab had already been tested in the morning and were now medicated and sleeping.

Gusev wasn't in the second lab either. A strobe light flashed constantly, causing the three men to squint against the blinding light. A man restrained against the wall was forced to endure the flashing lights. Alexi didn't seem to care, Turov smiled and the doctor flinched as they watched Sergi blinking and moving his head side-to-side trying to avoid the light.

The doctor explained that this laboratory was full of trigger mechanisms for the headaches. They used light, or sound, or barometric pressure changes on the subjects while attempting to start the headaches. The room was fully monitored, with cameras and microphones to pick up anything that was said.

The doctor didn't want to take them to the third laboratory, but wasn't enjoying the sight of his former boss chained to the wall, so he led them out of the room. Alexi was comfortable in the last laboratory, he didn't need explanations. This was the torture room. Once the headaches were in full swing the subject was brought here and the process of trying to extract useful information really began.

"Doctor Gusev, what are you doing? This is unacceptable!" Zolkin tried to push past Turov as they stepped through the door.

Gusev's subject was suspended in a harness in mid-air. He was just lowering the body when the interruption made him stop in surprise. The victim hovered just above the flame licking off the top of a portable construction space heater.

The doctor watched in horror, as Turov's arm barred his advance.

"What is wrong with what the young doctor is doing?" Alexi asked. "Is this not what I expected from you?"

Doctor Zolkin didn't hesitate, "No this is not acceptable, we can achieve our goals with normal, controlled, and sane experimentation. I can get the answers the proper way."

"Doctor, I'm really starting to wonder how much time you've wasted." He turned to the Gusev, "Continue."

They all watched as the young doctor started to lower the chain hoist. The victim's bound feet hit the flames and the unfortunate man's whole body twisted and shook as the subject tried to move out of the way. Then his feet touched the burner and the subject screamed. The smell of burning flesh hit them instantaneously. Alexi watched how long Gusev held the victim's feet in the flames before lifting them off again. He was interested as Gusev questioned the subject.

"What do you see? Tell me everything."

The subject was talking so fast and screaming for release that Gusev wasn't getting his answer. He lowered the subject's feet again until they touched the flame and held them there longer. Final the subject screamed out answers, describing his auras. This one was describing blind spots in his vision, which was nothing new, and Gusev obviously wanted more.

Alexi was impressed, he liked the young doctor's style. He wondered how much farther along they might be with the young doctor in charge instead of Zolkin.

"Doctor Gusev is there no more information to be had from this subject?"

"No sir, there is not. We need new subjects. We need different types than these ones we have here. These ones are all the same."

Alexi could hear the disappointment in the young doctor's voice, and smiled to himself.

"Don't worry, I will get you more subjects. Gusev, I am impressed." Alexi nodded, "Carry on with your experiments."

Alexi turned and headed out of the room, he didn't address Zolkin as he stalked down the hall with Turov at his heals.

Doctor Zolkin stared wide-eyed at Gusev as he backed out of the room, and quietly headed back to his office. He was going to have a breakdown. He needed to get out of this place.

He had been sitting at his desk for no more than ten minutes when three men showed up in his doorway. He had anticipated that this would be his end and had done the little he could to protect himself. Opening the desk drawer, he pulled out a large syringe loaded with a barbiturate tranquilizer. He had hoped it would allow him to save himself if it came to that.

It had. Now he tried moving around the desk to give himself some kind of chance with these trained men. One of the guards wasn't wasting time and drew out his gun. He shot the doctor as he attempted to maneuver around the side of his desk. The impact slammed the doctor against the wall. He slid down, dying quickly, the syringe still dangling from his hand. The head guard ordered the other two to pick up the doctor. Turov had instructed them to take him down in the incineration pile so they didn't miss the weekly truck.

Back in his office, Alexi had been sitting and thinking through the situation regarding the new woman. It was late when he walked to the window and stared out into the darkness. He had a feeling he was finally getting close to something, even if he still didn't know what that something was.

He felt a grin cross his face.

*****

The man Ivan had assigned to recon watched Septon's security truck doing their rounds through his night vision scope. Dressed in camo, well back from the road, there was no way they would ever spot him. After the truck passed he turned back to the offices and began making notes on a small pad using a pinpoint laser pen.

He watched the grin spread across on the old man's face. He thought that the old man wouldn't be smiling if he knew he was being watched. There was the full-face shot he needed.

Bingo! I got you now you motherfucker.

CHAPTER 19

Gary spent the night drifting in and out of sleep. He'd been going over the problem again and again. He was sure that Chantal had said something important. He kept coming back to her comment that the line sometimes reminded her of a line on a GPS laid out in front of her.

He couldn't understand what he was supposed to do with that. They all seemed to have visual auras. The blank spots, extra objects in front of their sight and now Chantal with a specific line. He sensed the answer was right there, but he still didn't see it.

The question that he kept asking was whether the directions or message was the same for everyone, or different between people. Was he supposed to use them all to get one answer, or were they all on individual tangents pointing to different solutions.

He could only think it must be one message for everyone, which opened another list of questions. Where had the message come from, and how long had they had it? How was he supposed to use these different visions?

He couldn't worry about that, he needed to stay on the message. Only two people had stopped by with headaches since yesterday, and Gary had asked all the questions he could think of, but the migraine sufferers never knew the why, or what, either.

But if the message was being projected through the vision, then maybe it was supposed to be projected onto something. He was stumped. About three a.m. his conversation with Chantal came back to him. She'd described a route, which made him think of a map.

Projecting the visions onto a map wasn't the dumbest idea. Perhaps it would be best to start with Chantal because of the clear line she'd described. The question was, what map?

Gary got up, dressed, and rousted around the kitchen making a pot of coffee. Even at that hour there were a few people about, including some who seemed to be taking guard shifts. He went for a walk, questioning anybody he came across. After managing to find a guy who had some maps, he borrowed a large one of the U.S.. The problem was at home, so he might as well start there.

Sitting beside Chantal, nursing his semi-cold coffee, he wondered how to go about it. Finally, as it inched closer to morning he nudged her. He let her wake up a bit before getting to the issue. "Chantal, I need you to help me test an idea,"

"Jesus, Gary, can you let me wake up? What do you want?" She rolled away, pulling the blanket over her head.

He knew he was walking a fine line, but it was the only way to get to the visions, "I need that line you always see. I want you to have a migraine."

"For God's sakes!" She laughed out loud. "Why?"

"Look Chantal, this whole thing centers around these visions. If I'm going to figure it out I'll need the visions. I figured because you have a specific one, that you were the best to start with, and if I'm going to ask people to get headaches on purpose, I should start with you."

"Great. Well, since you think it's so easy, just let me get a coffee and then I'll ask one to come out for you," she said sarcastically.

"Look, it's hard for me to ask people to do this. I don't want to be like Septon, but to stop them I've got to get to the bottom of this."

She sighed. "Just let me shower and eat. Then you can play around inside my head." She smiled at him as she got up and left to find a shower. He told her to find him near the newly constructed sleeping quarters.

He needed some time too. He had to find Dexter and get some things ready. He wanted one of the new rooms to use a private place to test the migraines.

"You can't do this man. You'll be just like them." Dexter seemed shocked.

"No, I won't keep anybody against their will, and I'll have the medications that they usually use to make the headaches stop. I promise I'll let them leave when they want to." He was serious when he turned to stare Dexter in the face. "There really is a message or something. I'm sure of it. The only way is to find out for sure, is to have the headaches and see the visions. You should be there for all the testing, so everyone feels there is a balance, and someone they can trust."

A reluctant Dexter helped pick a room and then headed out to round up the items on Gary's list. When he came back they went about making the room more closed in, private and darker. He plugged a couple of extension cords together and ran them into the room. The two men were just finishing up when Chantal arrived.

"So excuse me. Is this where you come to have your head played with?" Chantal had on a serious face, and Gary laughed.

"Yes, it is young lady, please come in and leave your twenty-five cents in the jar."

Dexter wasn't laughing. He stayed in the corner with his back to the wall. Chantal sat on the chair they had placed in the middle of the room. "I'm all yours."

He knew that she was stressed. They all were. Days of hiding, knowing people were after you, would do that. That was what was hard about being on the run. Usually you slipped up under the continuous pressure of thinking everyone you met was after you.

Since stress was one of the triggers for a migraine, he knew Chantal was already primed, just as the rest of the sufferers who were stuck in here would be. He was hoping that a migraine was close enough that one of her secondary triggers would send her over the edge.

Gary reached over and handed Chantal a bottle of red wine. She laughed, it was only ten in the morning. She laughed again when he handed her a chocolate bar. His research told him these items were usually considered triggers. He waited for Chantal.

"So we're going to sit here while I drink this wine and catch a buzz?" She questioned Gary.

"Pretty much."

"It might take a while doing it this way."

Dexter thought it was crazy. He couldn't believe they were trying to give her a headache. He watched the woman drinking down the wine like water and knew she'd regret it later. Then to his relief he watched Gary reach out and take it back. Dexter agreed, that had to be enough.

"Tell me when it starts, okay?"

"Oh, don't worry, I will."

Gary reached over and flipped on the ghetto blaster they'd found. It blared out some new music that was heavy on the guitars with lots of screaming vocals. Dexter had already stuffed plugs his ears because he'd been warned. Gary turned the volume up until the room started vibrating and kept an eye on Chantal.

She was clearly not as comfortable as she had been. Gary noticed she was blinking more and starting to squint. He reached over and threw a switch on the lamp. One of the men had gone out and swiped it from a construction site along-side the highway. Dexter had taken the red cover off, so now it flashed white strobes around the room.

The music pounded. Gary could see Chantal staring straight ahead, her hands were clenching open and closed. She licked her lower lip from one side to the other, leaned her head sideways and held it there. They all waited.

Chantal suddenly put her hand up. She felt the migraine coming on. Gary shut down the music and switched off the flashing light. He plugged in a normal lamp. Gary walked over to Chantal and asked her to stand as well.

"Do you see the line you told me about?"

"Yeah," Chantal cocked her head to the right. "The line is there."

"Does it hurt?"

"Not yet. I've got twenty or thirty minutes maybe." She gave him a smile, "let's get this over with. Okay?"

"Stand right here." He pointed to the wall where he had pinned up the map of the U.S.. He had to get her to explain what she was seeing if he was going to understand anything. "Okay, I see the line. Where do you want me to put it on the map?"

That was a good question. Gary knew that everything probably mattered here. How far away she stood from the map. Maybe even the scale of the map. "Tell me what you see. Does the line match anything?"

"The shape is the same as usual. It goes upwards to the left and then turns and makes a wiggly line straight up to almost the top of my vision." She gestured with her hands. "Right now that line is in the middle of the map starting around Texas, going northwest and then straight up towards North Dakota."

Nothing, thought Gary. How were you supposed to know the starting point, it could be anywhere. He paced across the little room, then back again. He turned to look at Chantal.

What if? What if you were supposed to start wherever you lived? That made more sense to him. Then the message would change depending on where you started. That might explain why Chantal said her line had changed before but had been stable for a few years.

Maybe the line was different before because she lived in Canada and was stable now because she'd been in New York for so many years. Gary had a lot of thoughts flashing at once. "Put the bottom of the line on New York. Have it start there."

Chantal was starting to struggle with the throb at the top of her eye socket, but moved to the right to adjust her vision so the line fell over New York. Now it went up and off the top of the map. "I'm not sure, it runs off the top of the map."

"Anything else? Does anything line up anywhere?"

Chantal stared at the map and wondered what she was looking at. Slowly she did see something that stood out. She moved herself slightly to the left and then stepped forward a half a step. She realized that was the wrong way and backed up a bit. "Shit!"

Gary stood beside her and stared at the map. He really wanted to see what she was seeing, "What?"

"This is crazy, but it seems to fit. I can adjust the line by moving right or left but it also gets bigger or smaller if I move backwards or forwards, which makes sense." She pointed at the map, "right now I have the line sitting perfectly on top of highway eighty-seven, leaving New York and going up through Albany. Gary, it sits on the road so perfectly that I can't believe it."

He was stunned. He'd been hoping – but to actually find a message or directions in a migraine…. He wanted to stop and think about it, but had to work with Chantal before her headache got so bad she had to stop, "Where does the line end Chantal? Where does it go?"

"Off the top of the map into Canada. I can't see where it ends up. If I move back I can get the end of the line on the map but it won't fall on the road like it does now."

"No don't move." He was thinking as hard as he could. "We need a North American map Dexter. Can you find the guy with the maps?"

Dexter didn't answer, but ran out of the room.

"Are you doing okay?" Gary put his arm around Chantal.

"No my head is really hurting. I need to take a pill now." She was pacing on the spot and getting aggravated.

Gary needed her to hang in there a bit longer, "Just a bit more sweetie, we're so close."

He was glad to see Dexter run back in. Quickly the two of them got the map unfolded and tacked up to replace the other one.

The men got out of the way and Chantal started looking at the new map. She had to back up a good two feet to adjust for the differing scale of this map. Then she moved around again to get the line started on New York, laying over top of the highway. She kept making small movements then stopped and took in a big breath, "Unbelievable."

"What now Chantal? What's there?"

"The line fits perfectly. It stops right on top of Montréal."

Bingo. Gary was thrilled with the fact they had solved something.

Now he knew he had to worry about Chantal. She needed to take her meds and lay down. He put a mark on the floor where she was standing.

She hadn't needed much encouragement and Gary walked her back to their area. He asked Dexter to keep the results to himself, until they could talk later and decide what to do with this new information. He sat there beside Chantal while she laid down, working things around in his head. Okay, a line to Montréal. What now? Were you supposed to follow it? Then what? Montréal was a big city, what would they do once they got there?

What about the visions that the other people were seeing? The blank spots or extra objects, how did they fit into the puzzle? Maybe they weren't part of it and only Chantal mattered. But he felt that this was all part of something bigger, and he had to figure out how it all fit together.

He knew that he would have to test the others and see where their objects showed up on the map and see how they added to Chantal's line. It also meant making headaches happen to a bunch of people, because he couldn't wait for them to arrive out of the blue. He left Chantal to sleep and went looking for Dexter.

*****

She woke Gary up around noon on Thursday. After being up half the night he was out like a log this morning. He was momentarily disorientated when he opened his eyes. Seeing Chantal standing there in their little area, it all came flooding back.

He'd spent the better part of the afternoon and night testing other visions and dealing with the other migraine sufferers. Surprisingly, most of them were intrigued enough to step up and participate. The results were consistent, which was good for Gary.

The ones who had blank spots and missing vision were, for some reason, the people with the migraines that were easiest to get going. Just sitting in the room was almost enough. The anxiety of what was coming had them teetering on the brink of a migraine, and they got there quickly.

The amazing thing was that they all had roughly the same blank spot. Some would have the spot shifted from one side to the other, but a couple of them had it in the exact same place. He was able to confirm that they all had the same message and saw the same things.

The blank spots were falling near the place where Chantal said her line ended. What was he supposed to do with this? What was it telling him?

Just the fact that they landed on the map so close to Chantal's line told him that these people were part of the same thing. Whatever that thing was.

Chantal's line seemed clear enough, you just start in New York and follow the line. But what could you do with the blank spots. Was that the endpoint? Were they expected to follow the line and then go to the blank spot? He had no idea.

That brought Gary to the people with extra things in their vision. He had a hell of a time getting these ones to start experiencing their headaches. They left the lights and music blasting for almost twenty minutes with the first one, he finally had started to throb just before they were ready to give up.

In the end the rest were consistent in what they saw, and he was left with another puzzle. Some seemed to have differing effects going on and saw things different than the others, but four of them saw the exact same thing. They described a bar that was narrow at one end and square at the other, like a pointer. When they all said the small point was landing on Montréal he hit pay dirt.

He was still confused. Why have a line going to a place if the pointer could do the same thing, and vice versa. It was obviously part of the message, just like the line and blank spots. It almost didn't matter how to use them if they all pointed to one location.

His morning coffee wasn't helping sort it out the confusion. He liked puzzles and solving problems, but this one had his adrenaline perking up, and he felt the pull take hold. They needed to follow the message.

CHAPTER 20

Ivan sat in the warehouse behind the dojo. He was thinking hard these days. Most of his daily business was being ignored while he worked full time on this Septon problem. In the end, if you have enough connections, or knew people in the right places who liked a little extra financial support, you could usually find out anything you wanted. Especially in less organized countries like Belize.

His team had come up with a name, and even supplied pictures. Ivan noticed immediately that the man was spending a lot of effort hiding his face. All the pictures showed long greying hair hanging down in front a face already obscured by a pair of glasses. He looked down at the new photos his recon team had delivered today, taken from the field across from Septon. More gray hair and not much of a face.

The name Alexi Tambov was certainly a fake. The question was, what was the real one? The second question was, what could he do with the information?

He'd already pulled the levers on his information network in Russia. His computer guys were tracing Tambov's footprints, but he knew they were only going to go back just so far and then the guy would disappear. But at least that would tell Ivan how long the man had been in hiding.

He wanted to just take the old man Tambov right off the street. He was sure if he could get the guy into a room, just the two of them, that he would get the answers he wanted.

He'd learnt not to rush the hard way, when he was a youngster. You needed to confirm the connections first. Find out who this Tambov was connected to, and what the consequences would be if you took him down.

There were always bigger fish to be wary of, and he was extra careful dealing with connections back in Russia. Gary had obviously stumbled onto something big. There was too much money tied up in that facility, and too much effort put into that hidden identity for this to be small time. It had taken a lot of planning, time, and patience.

So far all his team had been able to tell him was that this particular Alexi Tambov showed up around '92. He had no history before that. He wondered what the significance was that the Soviet Union had broken up in '91, and this guy, who is clearly Russian, gets a new name in '92.

Was he hiding something, or was he hiding from something? There were a lot of people who worked in government positions that lost jobs – hell the whole country lost jobs. That didn't make you change your name and hide halfway around the world.

Ivan's impatience had him taking his own phone calls.

"Slushayu." *Listening*, Ivan barked into the phone.

"You got time?" Gary wanted to know.

The excitement in Gary's voice amped up his own adrenaline. When Gary was excited there was usually some action on its way. "What's up?"

"I think I solved it. There is a message. It's directions actually. All the different symptoms work together to give you some kind of map to follow. It's fucking crazy."

Ivan was stunned. There was a map? He hadn't expected that. He figured there was another angle, blackmail, fraud, or ransom. Ivan has thought the facility was part of some money making scheme, but instead it actually was all experimentation to find a map. A map to where?

"Where does it go? What's the purpose?"

"I still don't know the purpose but I've got a location. It's Montréal, up in Canada."

Ivan wanted to stay on top of things, but too much was going on at once. He had been putting all his effort into Septon and had none left over for this bit of information. Somewhere in the back of his head he asked himself, who could have put messages inside a headache? Was that even possible? Could humans do that?

Ivan's brain did shift gears and his first thought made him laugh, he realized this phone call had a second meaning, "So when are you leaving?"

"As soon as I can. We're getting a team together, a truck, and some supplies." He stalled a moment, "Same as the old days Ivan – there's no sense in waiting when the answer is out there."

Ivan needed to think quickly, he couldn't order Gary around like one of his own men, but he also wanted to be part of the mission. He didn't want to be left out. Who knew what it was for, or what could be done with the information. He wondered if he could profit from it.

"Do you want some help, I could send a few men to shore up the group."

"I'm not sure Ivan, we'll need most of the room for the team because we can't get there without the visions."

It took Ivan a moment to realize what Gary was saying. Gary didn't believe the message ended in Montréal, he was making plans in case it went further. "You don't think Montréal is the target?"

"I'm having a hard time believing it's that easy. Things have been way too complicated and intense to be as simple as driving to Montréal."

Ivan agreed. He thought he was on to something big with Septon in his sights, now he was just as sure the message was big. It dawned on him that this Alexi guy had to know about the message to be searching for it in the first place. He wondered who else knew about it.

"How did Septon know about the message?"

"I've got no idea, but hopefully they don't figure it out for a while yet."

Ivan was sure they wouldn't be getting to it if he had anything to say about it. He just needed a bit more information and he was going to shut the bastards down. He was about to call it a night when the special cell phone rang in his inside pocket.

"Allo," he answered cautiously.

"Ivan Petrovski, I have heard good things about you."

He was instantly alarmed. His full name was being used again, this time by a voice that he didn't recognise. "Who is this? What do you want?"

"Easy Ivan. No need to be alarmed. You don't need to know me at this point. Just respect the fact that I have this phone number."

Okay, this is serious. "What is it you want?"

"Ah good, that is better. All I want is information. You made some requests this week. I wish to follow up on these questions."

Ivan was even more concerned now because his requests had brought this guy out, whoever he was. "I cannot answer your questions, because I don't know who you are." He didn't say, *and I don't know what side you're on.*

"I can assure you that you don't want to be on the other side Ivan. It will have to be enough knowing that that your bosses have given me the number. Why doesn't matter, just that they expect you to support my requests." The older voice spoke with authority, like someone used to giving orders.

Ivan knew that was the way it worked. People would show up unannounced and have a letter or mark that showed they had support from above and you would help as needed. It was the same way when Ivan needed work done elsewhere. He didn't have much choice.

"What help would you like?"

The man was very specific in what he wanted, and he took his time explaining his request. Ivan listened and agreed he could do it. Finally, he confirmed he would get back with answers to a number that the man supplied.

Now that he was off the phone, Ivan was trying to piece it together. His requests for information had come back blank, but this guy had come out of the woodwork and started asking questions. Someone else was very interested in this Alexi character running Septon.

Ivan prided himself on being on top of things and he didn't like being involved in something where he was behind the eight ball, but that's exactly where he was. Gary was off pursuing the message. Now someone in Russia knew more about this whole thing than he did, and was jerking his strings.

With tomorrow Friday, he knew he had to act fast. He called Victor over. Ivan was sure of one thing, this could be big. Whoever was calling from Russia had be up near the top and could be a very useful contact in the future if things worked out here.

CHAPTER 21

Friday morning marked two weeks since the first migraine support meeting. Gary was getting ready to tackle Chantal. She had to be the first one on the team and he wasn't sure how she would take his plan. She hadn't wanted to go to the meetings in the first place, and he'd talked her into them. Now here they were living in hiding, and hadn't been home in a week.

Gary waited until she finished her cigarette and was comfortably wrapped around a cup of coffee. "You ready to get out of here?"

Chantal saw the half-smile so she wasn't sure if he was serious. "To go home? Absolutely."

"I was hoping you would be interested in a road trip."

"Are you crazy? Why do we need to go to Montréal?" She shook her head at him.

"I think it's the only way we're going to stop Septon. We only figured out that it exists. We haven't figured out what it's all about."

"Why us? Why do we have to be the ones to figure it out?"

"Haven't you wondered about this? Who could put a message in your head? Don't you want to know why?" It wasn't something he could explain in his world.

"Are you sure this will work?"

He'd been sure she would go for it. Gary explained what he wanted her to get ready for the trip. She made some notes on what they needed and headed out to work on the list.

He knew he had to talk with Dexter. Sure enough, the big man was in the back relaxing with some of his men. Gary thought the guy needed to have more of a purpose than being resolved to staying in here. They had to want it to end as well.

When Dexter saw Gary walking down the corridor, he got up and moved over to an empty table.

*****

Alexi was the first one sitting in the conference room for the weekly management meeting. Turov was the last one in. The new operations manager slapped his laptop and a file on the desk. Alexi felt like this new blood brought more energy to the table and he liked that.

He was ready to start, but a car accident on the way to work this morning had him slightly on tilt. Something wasn't quite right about the whole thing. He and his driver had been in a minor fender bender while driving down Shore Drive in the Lincoln SUV.

They had both noticed the guy and his wife had been driving too close behind. It was pretty obvious in the mirrors that the couple were having a rather animated argument. His driver got caught flat-footed by a big delivery truck at one intersection and stopped abruptly for a yellow light.

Alexi had known what was coming as the car behind squealed its tires trying to stop, but still managed to hit the back of the SUV. That wasn't a big deal, it happened in New York every minute. It was what happened after that bothered him. The driver left his car and came to the passenger window.

Strange, but maybe the guy didn't want to stand on the road, which was a smart thing in New York, because you'd be run over. When Alexi had rolled the window down the guy had wanted to exchange insurance information.

Usually his people took care of these things, but the driver explained the paperwork was in the glove box, so, unsure of what to do next, he had gotten the paper out and handed it over. The guy had taken down some information and given it back.

Nothing else had happened and they had continued on their way. He had a feeling that something else had been going on there, but couldn't place it. But Alexi never ignored his feelings. They'd served him well over the years. For now he shook the incident off and looked around the table. "Well Doctor Gusev, what can you report on your new department."

"I have reviewed all the subject files. I am aware of their different types of symptoms. With a little time and some new subjects I will find out what these visions mean. I am sure of it." Gusev hit a note somewhere between confident and cocky.

"What will you do differently than our friend Doctor Zolkin?"

"Everything. He gave medications too quickly. I don't believe we will need any medications at all going forward. I don't think we should be stopping the headaches."

"Go on."

"We only applied certain techniques to bring about the headaches. Most times he didn't push hard enough. The doctor's limits were too low. I believe we can bring these visions quicker with some new tools. I will ensure the subjects have sufficient numbers of headaches to study."

"Excellent." He turned to Turov who seemed to be enjoying his new job as number-two, "What updates have you got?"

"I have more trained men ready who are clear on the mission. I've added security outside the perimeter, and in strategic locations throughout the industrial park, around the clock."

He shuffled a piece of paper, "We have street people with copies of pictures looking for our friends that keep getting in the way. The two black guys are at the top of our list. Pictures of the woman and her companion are circulating as well."

Alexi figured that was it and was about to speak when Turov continued, "There have been attempts over the last twenty-four hours to infiltrate out computer systems which we have successfully deflected. I am trying to figure out who is making these attempts. With the net I have out, it's just a matter of time."

Alexi didn't like the news about the cyberattack, and he immediately went back to this morning's incident. HE was sure someone was after him. He wondered about the accident again and decided Turov could to do something, "Turov, I want my SUV checked for bugs and tailing devices."

"Already done, sir. Before you leave and when you come in."

Proactive, good. He liked it in both of them. These men were up to the task. He stayed behind as they left the meeting room. He felt he was on the edge of a breakthrough, but today that prickly feeling that told him he needed to be watching his back as well.

Alexi opened up the single folder he had brought to the meeting. He had planned to get Turov to step up the research on this guy, but on further thought, decided to do it himself. It paid to keep some things to yourself. Never let the underlings see the whole process, whether it's going good or bad.

He opened the file and stared at the picture of Gary Collins. He wasn't even the target, he didn't have headaches, but that didn't ease Alexi's concern. This Collins was a successful man. A fixer, who had the reputation of solving things he put his mind to.

Collins was now missing. He hadn't been home in a week, had fallen off the radar. He had to be wondering what it the hell was going on with the two failed kidnapping attempts. Alexi knew this was the type of man who would never let it go. It was his bad luck to have someone like this stumble onto his research. How much could the hacking attempt and the disappearances of the soldier and cleaner be tied to Collins?

CHAPTER 22

Gary needed to be confident and in control. He knew that in the end the team needed to see him as a competent leader before they would agree to leave with him.

He had been impressed with almost all the people he had met in the shelter but knew he couldn't take everyone. Nor did he want to have to watch out for them all. A small team would be best, two vehicles at the most. He'd gone over it again and again, and couldn't get around the second truck. There just wouldn't be room for everybody in one vehicle after you added in the supplies they'd need.

He figured they would need two of each person. Two blank spot auras, two with extra objects, and two soldiers. Chantal and Gary would round out the group. Hers would be the only aura that wasn't backed up. There was nothing he could do about that. Then he needed to choose a team that could work together without friction.

The group in front of him was ready. The two women had blank spots at the exact same spot on the map. Vanessa Williams was a thirty-year old black woman who was a little over-weight, with attitude to burn. She was good natured, cocky and confident.

Mary Gardner was sixty-five years old, but still young at heart; feisty and intelligent. Gary had seen through her. She was rock steady. Gary watched her sitting on one of the chairs with her hands folded on her lap. Vanessa's cockiness and Mary's stability would help if he had to force more headaches.

The biggest problem facing the trip was passports. Gary's questions during the testing and walking around talking with people over the last week had also affected the team selection. He hoped that Vanessa had her passport, because she went back to the Caribbean every once in a while. Mary should have hers, because she had family all over the world she supposedly visited.

The man and teenager were there because they had the exact same visions of extra objects that were clearly lined up on Montréal. If they needed further migraines he knew the extra-object sufferers took more aggravation to get their headaches going and wanted guys he knew he could push.

Mike Mannon was twenty-eight. He didn't stay in the shelter full time, but since he'd lost his girlfriend to Septon, he kept coming in and spending time with the folks there. Gary knew that Mike felt guilt at skipping that one meeting when Septon grabbed his girlfriend. He could relate to how he would've felt if he'd lost Chantal. Mike was a global gypsy who was sure to have travel documents, since he spent part of last winter in Mexico.

The teenager was there with his mother, because Gary had wanted her to be present. The Somali boy hadn't been in the U.S. long. At fourteen, Geedi Egal was tall and lanky. He'd been calm during the testing, but Gary could tell the kid was going to explode if he stayed cooped up inside the shelter much longer. There was something in the kid's eyes that got to him. Now as he announced his selections, those dark eyes were locked onto him, carefully watching his every move. The new immigrants were sure to have passports.

Gary couldn't allow the kid to come unless his mother agreed, and he was worried about that. He wouldn't be able to answer the questions she was going to have, but hoped he'd get through to her somehow.

Deuce stood in the back with Dexter. Gary didn't know what Dexter had told Deuce, but it didn't matter, because he had to explain the whole plan to everyone. And it was time.

"Okay. I'm going to be straightforward with this. You all saw the results of your testing, and you all know that there are some bad people out on the streets trying to figure out what these visions mean."

Gary watched a few heads nod, and made sure everyone was with him, "I put all your results together, and I'm sure there is a message there. In my opinion it's directions to somewhere, or something."

He used the map to show them where each person's visions showed up. He explained that he wasn't sure what the blank spots and extra pieces meant right now, but that they fell onto the map meshing with Chantal's line, which seemed to be important.

"We know you are all in danger out there. At least one group is willing to kidnap and probably torture people to try and find this message. How many more other groups are trying as well?"

He paused for emphasis, "I think we need to follow this message, or its directions, and solve this puzzle before they do. It's the only way we can be sure that that we are safe. I think it's the only way for us all to get out of here."

"I want this group to make up the team. We'll make sure we have all the supplies we need, and will take all the precautions we can to be safe out there."

He could tell they were all in their own thoughts. In their place he would be too, he was asking a lot of them. Perhaps more than they realized.

Mike was the first to speak up, "I'm sick of this going on. I need a change. And as much as I want to help these folks here, hanging around doing nothing isn't bringing her back," he scratched his head, "so I guess I'm in."

"Exactly, you hit the nail on the head," Mary was a quick second, "I've had it with hiding here. I want out too. I'll do it."

Gary was encouraged. He hadn't expected to get any answers right away. He'd planned on asking them to sleep on it. This was better than he'd thought.

Vanessa had been unsure, but seeing the other two jumping in got her to thinking. There might be some shopping on the way. And clearly there were no eligible bachelors in the shelter. Maybe this was the change she needed. "I think this little journey you have planned might be a bit of fun."

With three of them on board Gary looked at the Somali woman and explained why she was there, "I have asked you to be here out of respect for your son's age. I will only ask him to come if we have your blessing in advance."

The woman was quiet and didn't answer for a few moments. She was beaming with pride, her head held high as a tear formed in the corner of her eye. Gary held his breath.

"The name Geedi means traveler. It is his destiny. You have my blessing." She patted her son on his arm.

Gary looked at Geedi. The fire burning in the kid's eyes was evidence of what he thought about the whole idea. "I would be honoured to go on a trip of discovery," he said in his softly accented English.

Gary had to take a second. *A journey of discovery.* The kid had put it perfectly. Moving on to the next step, he talked about the plan to head to Montréal, and basically take it wherever it led from there. He confirmed everyone's passport situations. Although a few would have to go home to get them, they would all be ready for the next morning. Saturday.

Looking at the back of the room Gary addressed everyone, "Well the only thing left to decide is whether Deuce is coming with us. What do you think Deuce?"

*****

Deuce hadn't been ready for that. As he listened to everyone else, he had been wishing he was going. After fighting this battle for years, he was sure his sister was long gone. He could keep getting petty revenge in the day-to-day street battles, or he could consider beating the bastards to the end and stop them once and for all. He looked quickly at Dexter who shrugged his shoulders, as if to say that it was all right with him.

"No question dude. I'm in."

"Okay then, we're a go. Any questions, come and see me. Use tonight to sort your things and get some sleep. We leave in the morning if everything is ready." Gary motioned Dexter to stay behind as the others filed out. He wanted an update on the two trucks, one set up with supplies and headache triggers. The other truck needed to have passenger seats and more supplies. They would be leaving early.

He had to call Ivan.

CHAPTER 23

Gary wanted to make a quiet exit, but there was no denying the others the opportunity to see the team off. Everyone was hoping the team could end their collective ordeal by beating Septon to solving the puzzle. They surrounded the two trucks, patting shoulders and hugging the travellers.

Dexter had done a good job, the two trucks looked like new. The first thing Gary had done was check for insurance paperwork. Dexter had been there and assured him the trucks would pass inspection. Gary didn't know whose trucks they were, but hoped they were borrowed with permission.

The Escalade would carry six of them. The high-roofed cargo van held most of their supplies and baggage.

Gary slowly herded the team into the SUV. He would do the driving. They were waiting for someone. It had taken him a while to get Dexter to allow someone new to come to the shelter. When one of Dexter's men shouted that someone was there, they all watched as the garage door slid open. One of Ivan's trucks rolled in and pulled to a stop beside the cargo van.

Out of the corner of his eye he could see Dexter flexing his shoulders and clenching his fists. Before anyone could comment, Gary stepped forward and stuck out his hand, "Ivan, glad you could make it."

"Hey." Ivan looked at the people sheltering behind the Escalade. He settled on Dexter. "So these are the people you're helping?"

"Let me introduce you." Gary introduced Ivan and Victor to Dexter and Deuce.

"Victor isn't too happy about going," Ivan explained, "but he will do this for me, and for you."

Gary understood the meaning. If Ivan instructed Victor to help him then Victor would do whatever he had to for Gary. That was what their code expected.

Gary eyed Victor, "I hope you will realize this is an important trip. All the people here will feel better with your skill and strength along for the ride, including me."

The nod that Victor gave made him feel that the man was going to take the job seriously. He knew that the price of Victor's presence was that Ivan would be given regular updates on their progress. There would be no hidden agendas here. Gary looked around, "It's time to go. Victor, you'll be in the van with Deuce."

Victor grabbed a couple of heavy bags out of Ivan's vehicle and slung them into the back of the cargo van. Gary wanted to say something about the bags, because he could guess what was in them, but then thought better of it. They might need all the help they could get at some point. This was forcing a conscious decision, there would be no cops, he realized they would only stop the process. The team would be seeing this one through themselves.

Ivan stood beside the Escalade. "I am close to figuring out this Septon thing. I'll keep on it."

"We'll keep in touch. We may need your help along the way." He stuck out his hand, "and thanks for Victor."

"Victor has been with me a long time, I trust him like I trust you. And yes, I'll help you any way I can." The two men shook hands through the open window.

Gary looked at Dexter for a second then spoke, "Keep these people safe just a bit longer Dexter."

"I hope you'll find whatever it is Gary. I know you won't give up, so good luck."

Gary took a big breath, looked at Chantal and then back at Dexter.

"All right Dexter, let's open up that door. We're out of here."

The garage door swung open and the two trucks moved through it, over the curb and onto the street. They were in no hurry, and casually made their way north to the top of Brooklyn where they would cross into Manhattan and then cross again onto the mainland at Weehawken and the 30th Street Bridge. They needed to get the Garden State Parkway up to Highway eighty-seven. Then it was a one-way trip to Montréal.

Mary sat in the back seat, a brightly coloured scarf wrapped around her grey curls, nails and make-up done like she was headed out for a night on the town. She smiled, "It's about time we got this show on the road."

*****

The man watching the warehouse had only been there twelve hours.

His orders were to make note of any activity coming or going, and report back to Turov. He knew something big was up when two trucks came out of the back garage and roared down the road. The tinted windows on the Escalade made it tough, but he was sure the woman's companion was driving. The black guy driving the cargo van was definitely one of the ones on his watch list.

He now had two of the targets exiting the scene in trucks and had to decide what to do. Keep watching the warehouse, or follow the vehicles. The man sprinted to his own car and flipped a U-turn, racing up the road to catch the trucks.

He placed his call back to headquarters and was told to hold. Turov came onto the phone, "What do you have?"

"Movement, it looks like the woman's companion is driving one of two trucks that left the warehouse. The black man you are searching for is driving a second one."

Using Sergi's files, Turov had found the warehouse just in time by the looks of it.

"Where are you now?"

"Almost in Manhattan. The two trucks are keeping together, headed north."

"Don't lose them. Is that clear?"

"Yes sir."

Turov placed a call down to the garage. He wanted a team on the road immediately to catch up. He couldn't let them get wherever they were going. He also needed to update Alexi. When he found his boss in his office, Alexi became very interested.

"Where are they? When did they leave?"

"They are heading into Manhattan in two vehicles. They must be transporting a number of people, or else why the two trucks?"

Exactly. Did they figure it out? Was this Collins guy going after the message? Alexi knew the answer and kicked into gear. "You have teams on the road?

"Yes sir, six men in one SUV in addition to the car that saw them leave, and is now following."

"As soon as the backup crew arrives I want them to confirm how many people are in the vehicles, and who they are."

"Yes sir, I'm on it."

In the garage Turov walked among his men, making sure their preparations were perfect. He watched the guns being checked and the supplies of ammo being loaded into the truck.

He took Petrov, the new crew leader, aside. There was no room for error in this operation. Turov knew that Alexi would be holding everyone accountable. This meant that Turov would do the same thing. "You are clear how much I want this woman?"

"Yes sir."

"Good. There will be no excuses. I will only accept success." Turov was sure the man knew what was expected from him. The crew leader returned to his men as Turov stood near the door, arms crossed, watching them complete their preparations.

They would be using a black van because that was the only colour Septon had. Turov thought about that, and realized that the targets would probably recognise the van from previous run-ins. Damn, he should have had some other vehicles brought in.

His men looked tough. These were all trained soldiers that Turov knew had previous combat experience of some sort or another. The ones he'd brought in recently were especially tough. He knew that if some of Sergi's remaining men were hesitant, the new soldiers would take over completely and get the job done.

Turov took a deep breath as the van backed out of the garage.

*****

Alexi had taken a pill. At his age, anger and excitement were hard on the heart. Since Turov had left his office he'd been emotional. There really was a message. Even though he knew it existed, and had been after it for years, the reality of it all still shocked him.

He'd had a worrying question back in the beginning and now that it was finally unfolding he had it again. Who could put messages in someone's head? That was the real question that drew him to this, why he had spent years hiding and amassing the fortune necessary to build the facility, and run the experiments.

Someone else figuring it out and beating him to the answer was unacceptable. It could not be allowed to happen. The adrenaline and anger were mixing, and it was getting the better of him. The pill should calm him down, but right now he just wanted to explode.

Alexi rubbed his forehead for a moment, then he slid his fingers around to his temples and squeezed a bit before doing little circles with his fingers. There was an irony to it all, Alexi had been suffering his own headaches since university. He dealt with it in his own way.

The irony wasn't that he had the headaches, it was that he knew that the message was in his head, but would rather get it out of someone else. Then Alexi thought of the cameras that Turov had mentioned. He found himself lowering his hand from his head, even if it was his own facility.

*****

The backup crew from Septon kept in touch with the car following the targets. The van's driver kept the gas pedal pinned to the floor to catch up.

They were almost up to the state line. They had been moving fairly well now on highway eighty-seven. The crew knew the highway went north through New York State all the way to the Canadian border. They also knew that Turov would want the hit outside New York City if possible. Across state lines was the best. They were always to keep things clean and professional.

By the time they caught up to the car that had been tailing the subjects, they were well past Albany into the northern part of the state. They let the car's driver know they were there and instructed him to close in on the two vehicles. He slowly gained on the two targets, passing casually in the fast lane.

Once he was ahead of them, he slowed gently and let the two trucks slowly gain on him until they were right behind and forced to pass. By the time the vehicles had passed he'd had a good look into both of them.

He placed a call to the back-up team and Petrov phoned Turov, "We have them in our sights now. We're certain the woman is there, her companion is driving. It looks like there are three or four more in that truck. The cargo van behind has the black man and a second guy who looks pretty tough."

"Okay, the van must be muscle. It's the Escalade and the woman we want."

"Yes sir."

The crew and the single driver in the following car stayed back, waiting for a chance to do something. It finally happened an hour later, when the two vehicles in front pulled off the interstate and rolled into a rest stop. The crew leader figured they were no more than an hour from the border, so this was the place.

He instructed the car's driver to block the van as it left the parking lot and keep those two out of the picture. Then Petrov would block the truck when it tried to get back on the road. Everything should be done quickly. Both of the Septon vehicles pulled in to the lot, staying to one side.

*****

Gary finished stretching and got into the Escalade. Turning his head, he watched Deuce climbing into the cargo van. Everyone ready, he started towards the exit. Looking in the mirror he noticed the two vehicles parked on the edge of the lot. The one seemed to be the same car which had passed them earlier, then slowed until they passed him back. His instincts were telling him something, and he checked the side mirror again.

The car pulled ahead as soon as Gary pulled out. It parked at an angle, which blocked in Deuce's parked cargo van. Suddenly the other vehicle sitting along the edge of the lot accelerated towards the Escalade.

Gary glanced out the side window as the black van passed. *Shit,* he thought to himself, *a black van.* Before he could take another breath, the van turned and slammed on its brakes right in front of him. He was already reacting. You don't stop no matter what. That was another thing he'd learnt in foreign countries. You don't stop.

Gary gunned the accelerator and swung the truck left. The Escalade missed the back of the van by a foot and bounced hard as it jumped the little retaining wall that ran around the parking lot. He kept the gas pedal pinned as the truck chewed grass, tearing through some shrubs, before slamming down into the ditch.

Everyone was banging around inside the SUV, holding on for dear life. Vanessa screamed while Chantal swore softly in French. Gary fought the wheel as the ditch grabbed them. He wrestled the truck straight and they flew up the other side of the bank.

The Escalade lifted off the ground, gaining a little air as it left the ditch, and everything was still for a moment until the tires hit the road. The truck bounced and swerved, tires squealing as he got the vehicle straightened out. Finally in control, racing down the road, Gary took the time to look back to see what was happening behind them.

He couldn't see rest stop, but the black van had gotten straightened out and was trying to catch up. Gary kept the pedal down as the Escalade neared the speed limit. He would welcome the cops now. He watched the needle as it kept climbing. They would outrun the black van, or the cops would pull them over for speeding. The way he saw it, either way was golden.

*****

Deuce and Victor had been floored when the little car pulled in front of them. What was the fucker doing blocking them in like that? Deuce leaned on his horn and then started to back up to go around the guy. Victor was rolling down the window to tell the guy where to go when someone jumped out of the car. They saw the gun in the guy's hand at the same moment.

Then they noticed the Escalade swerving sideways up ahead and crashing over the little wall. Victor realized before Deuce did that it was a hit, shouting, he pointed at the car, "Ram it."

Deuce wasn't a trained soldier, but he'd done his time on the streets and didn't hesitate. Hesitation killed. He jammed the shifter into low and nailed the gas. The van surged forward. The driver's eyes reacted to their move. He hadn't expected them to go on the offensive, thinking they would try to back up and drive around.

The van slammed into the car, which slid sideways, hitting the man with the gun trying to intercept them, and knocking him to the ground. Deuce couldn't see if the guy was injured, but really didn't care as he kept pushing the car until it swung to the side and they pushed through it.

Deuce looked at Victor, "Shit, I wonder where they are?"

"We'll catch them," Victor pointed up the road in the Escalade's direction. Deuce put his boot down on the pedal and they raced to catch up.

*****

Roaring down the interstate, Gary watched the needle as he passed seventy, then eighty miles an hour. He could take it to the limit if he was by himself, but he had the others to think about, and knew that this was probably scaring them all. He didn't have much choice though. He thought the next break they would get would be at the border thirty minutes away.

He was sure the van was keeping up, but he wasn't getting a long enough of a straightaway to see, as the road twisted and turned around the mountains. He'd been using both lanes, cutting the corners to keep his speed up the best he could.

When they got stuck behind a bunch of transport trucks, Gary knew the black van would catch up. He watched the rear view mirror as they appeared, gaining quickly on the Escalade. Finally spotting a break, he pulled out, passing two transports, but the damage was done. The black van was right behind them and would be right on top of them once it got by the big trucks.

A straightaway didn't help and Gary watched the black van pass the trucks. Now it was coming up behind them. He had to make a call. He could accelerate again but with them so close he didn't like the idea of something happening at high speed. He thought he'd rather have a bit more control. So he sped up, but didn't nail it. The van was still coming fast.

Gary had one more decision to make. Let them pass or not. Once they were in front he lost some degree of control, and would be relegated to reacting to whatever they did. That wasn't what he wanted. He wondered how far these guys were willing to go in broad daylight, but figured he'd find out shortly.

The van came flying up behind the Escalade and pulled out to pass. Gary was already moving into that lane, and the black van had to brake or swerve. It chose to brake. He straddled the middle of the lanes and waited for their next move.

Suddenly the van rammed into the rear of the Escalade. Gary felt the vehicle surge forward and fought for control. He heard Vanessa scream again. He took a quick look at the passengers in the back to make sure they were okay. Mary staring straight ahead looking rather serene through it all, while Vanessa looked hysterical, swivelling her head left and right trying to see what was coming next. Mike was watching through the back window and Geedi was staring back at him in the mirror calmly watching what he was doing.

Gary thought they would be taking out the tires sooner than later. He needed a new plan and quick. He didn't have time for the ringing cell phone. "Chantal get that, put it on speaker."

"Gary, it's Deuce. We have you guys in sight. We're coming up strong. What do you want to do?"

"You guys are alright?"

"Sure man, but the front of the truck is done in. It won't get us across the border."

Shit. He hadn't planned on that. He wondered how bad the back end of the Escalade was. It did make some things easier though. If they were going to have to change vehicles anyway, then they could do some more damage to these ones if that's what it would take.

"I'm going to try and get these guys going from side-to-side trying to pass us. Do what you can from behind. Sound good?"

"Sure boss, I'll be there."

Gary moved the vehicle to one side, and the black van jumped to pass. He swung in front of them, and the black van veered back the other way. Anticipating the move, he was already turning the steering wheel back, and the Escalade cut them off again.

When the Septon crew threw the black van back to the left a second time, the motion was a little more violent, and the van rocked. That was when Deuce hit them. Accelerating in the passing lane as the black van pulled left, trying to straighten itself out, Deuce turned right and clipped the back of the van.

Deuce was thrown out of control but had expected it, and was strong-arming the van around straight before it even started to lose traction. He fish tailed down the gravel on the shoulder of the road, before pulling back onto the asphalt and racing after Gary.

The black van hadn't expected the attack from the rear, and the driver was caught off guard while fighting the momentum of his own quick turn. He was jarred and shoved forward. Before he realized what was happening, the black van was going all the way around and he was fighting to keep the top-heavy vehicle from rolling.

The black van slid backwards and hit the ditch awkwardly. The driver tried to keep it straight as it went in, but the van bounced once, turned, then almost rolled over before coming to a stop with its bumper dug into the grass on other side of the ditch.

The men shook themselves off and climbed out of the van. An inspection told them they were good to go, and they were pushing the van out in minutes. They knew they had missed their chance and had little time to try again.

The phone rang a few times but Petrov ignored it. This wasn't the time to be giving anyone an update. When the Escalade reached the border town of Champlain, Petrov knew the targets must be trying to leave the States. He was sure there was no way they had crossed yet because the vehicles had too much damage, just like his did.

He dropped two of his men off with a phone near the border crossing's line-up and went looking around the town for the damaged trucks. His men left at the border were checking any small trucks and multi-passenger vehicles. They were instructed to look in the back for other people.

When something about a passenger van caught his eye, the soldier kept looking at the old woman who was driving. For some reason she reminded him of someone, but he couldn't place her. She was alone in the front of the van holding tight to the steering wheel, looking straight ahead. With all the tinted windows he couldn't see inside the back.

People moving wasn't unusual, and he watched a rental van with an animated black woman at the wheel move up the line. He could see her talking away and reaching over to grab her male friend. She sure looked like she was having fun.

The soldier looked back at the old woman as her vehicle was about to go through the crossing. He looked back at the second rental as it passed directly in front of him. He hadn't been able to get a look at the guy in the passenger seat who was fending off the black woman with his arms up by his face.

When the soldier saw the guy's arms drop as the van went by, he knew he had them, but it was too late. The man in the passenger seat was the one who had been staring out the back window of the truck they'd tried to run off the highway. The targets had switched vehicles and now they were into Canada.

Petrov got the phone call and raced to the crossing, but he couldn't do a thing. They didn't have passports to get into Canada. More importantly, they had no passports to get back into the U.S.. Shit – most of his crew didn't have the paperwork to be in the U.S. in the first place.

He couldn't put it off any longer, he knew he had to call Turov with the news.

CHAPTER 24

The first thing the team did after they were across the border was change drivers, so Gary was now at the wheel. He'd seen Septon's crew watching the lines at the border crossing, and knew they couldn't do anything there. What were they going to do? Draw guns in broad daylight right next to armed border guards, and start shooting? Not likely.

Septon knew the trucks they were driving, so until they changed vehicles again they needed to hide. They were on Quebec provincial highway fifteen, headed for Montréal. They were going to need a place to hide, and he didn't want to use a hotel. Septon would be all over them.

Gary dialled while he drove. He heard Ivan answer, "Da."

"It's me. Septon hit us before the border. We got away, but had to change vehicles. They saw us crossing and know what we're driving. Can you get us someplace secure outside Montréal so we can sort out some new vehicles and figure out what the deal is here?" Gary hated asking for favours but assumed Ivan had contacts everywhere.

"Let me see what I can do. I'll get back to you."

Everyone in the rental had been pretty quiet since the attack. He was surprised when Mary was the first one to say something.

"It was everything I could do to not ram that guy, and drive over the bastard right in front of the border guards."

He reminded himself not to get her mad. He turned to Vanessa, "How about you guys?"

"Oh, I seen them and was getting scared, but once Mike started saying those nice things to me, I felt everything settle right down." Vanessa turned to a red-faced Mike, "I liked the things you were saying about my hair and eyes."

She'd obviously had fun driving the second truck.

Mike turned even redder if that was possible. "I was just trying to distract you from the guy."

Everyone laughed as Vanessa reached over to squeeze his thigh again. Gary saw Chantal pull her cigarettes out of her purse and stick them in the pocket of her jean jacket. He had better plan on pulling over soon to give them all a five-minute break.

Gary wondered about Geedi, he hadn't said much through the whole thing, "You hanging in there Geedi?" Gary watched in the rear view for his response.

"Everything's good Gary. I just hope we get to run into those guys again."

Another one who was ready to go at Septon instead of being scared. Mary and Geedi, Gary shook his head. Thankfully his phone rang, "Gary, it's Ivan."

"You got something for us?"

"Yes. But do me a favour and keep this message to yourself. You don't need to mention it to any of the people you're going to meet." He gave Gary a phone number and told him they would receive instructions to a warehouse in one of the suburbs of Montréal.

"Thanks, I'll be in touch."

Gary placed the call and Ivan's contact gave them instructions to cross the Champlain Bridge towards Montréal. Then they were directed to an industrial park in Verdun, a suburb in the southeast end of the city. When Gary found the place, there was a car parked outside the front door.

A big guy in a dark suit looked around suspiciously as he climbed out of his car. He looked like a mobster. Gary stepped out of the van to speak with him. The mobster kept looking into the van, like he was having a hard time understanding why a couple guys, a bunch of ladies and a black man would be involved in anything that needed his kind of help. As he handed over some keys and codes for the security system, he assured Gary the place would be empty for the weekend, and that workers wouldn't be in until Monday morning. That was fine with him, he didn't plan on being there any longer than necessary.

They had ditched Victor's guns at the border, much to his disapproval, but Gary couldn't take the chance the Canadian border guards would use the hardware as an excuse to turn them back. He asked the mobster about guns, then called Victor over and let the two men work out the details.

Before he left, the mobster explained that one of his men would be watching the building to make sure no one bothered them, but that the guard would leave them alone. Gary was impressed. Ivan had found them a spot, and the people he found would watch over them while they were in Montréal. There was nothing better than having connections.

*****

The team drove the vans into the loading dock where they were out of view. Inside, the cafeteria was big enough for them to spread out in, and everyone got comfortable. There was nothing to do but get some rest and shed some of the adrenaline of the day.

Chantal immediately grabbed a smoke and wandered out into the open warehouse. Jesus, she needed one of these. What a day. She tried not to feel guilty that this was all about her, but she knew Septon really wanted to see her auras. She felt a little bad about dragging the others all over the country, but like Gary had said, everyone's visions are part of the message. The problem was, what goddamned message?

She was startled when she realized Mary was standing beside her.

"He has no idea where we're going does he?" she asked.

Chantal shook her head, "No. He has no clue."

"That's alright. Men like him don't let go of these kind of things. He'll get us there."

"It's that stubborn streak that worries me. He won't give up and will keep pushing."

"That's not stubborn. That's character and a strong one at that. He's a keeper."

She looked hard at Mary. The old woman was giving her advice. Finally she stubbed out her smoke and started to head back to the team. Mary reached out and touched her arm, "I'll take one of those things if you don't mind."

"I didn't know you were a smoker Mary."

"I haven't been for a long time, but today I realized that cigarette smoke isn't the most dangerous thing out there, and besides my nerves need a little calming."

Chantal paused at the warehouse door and looked back at Mary. The woman was just standing there having her cigarette, staring off into space. Chantal wondered what she was thinking.

Back in the cafeteria, everyone else was sitting around. Deuce had dragged a couple of nice chairs in from the lobby and there was a couch against one of the walls. Not much, but it would do. Gary asked Deuce to take a drive and bring back a bunch of take-out, so everyone could get some food into them.

Gary needed to think, he needed to decide what to do next, and excused himself to take a walk. What he really needed to do was loosen up, his body was strung tight. He found some open space in a corner and started to work through an exercise series.

He liked to train while he thought. The combination of control and rhythm would sort his head out. He began with some basic Sambo moves, letting his body flow to full extension while he kicked and punched at the air. Muscles lengthened and loosened as he warmed up. He could feel his energy returning as the blood pumped through his veins.

Gary's fluid movements fluctuated between slow and deliberate steps and lightning fast, explosive attacks. Balance was extremely important, and at one point he just held a pose, balancing on his right foot while holding the left stationary out to the side at head-height.

Working on his control, he let the leg come down and then raised it right back up it the air, and held it there. Gary forgot about the day. He focused on the moves.

Swinging an elbow back at an imaginary person, he noticed Geedi standing off to the side. The boy must have followed him into the warehouse.

"Hey Geedi, what's up?"

"Nothing. I was just watching what you were doing. What type of martial art was that?"

"Russian Sambo. It's a combat fighting technique."

"Could you teach me?"

Gary wondered why he wanted to learn. Some people just liked to fight and like to pick on people, while others just want to be able to defend themselves. Some liked the exercise and discipline required to train. Gary thought Geedi might be in the second group.

"Why would you like to learn the techniques? Do you like to fight?"

Geedi stepped closer like he wanted Gary to see his face clearly. He hesitated, "I don't want to hurt people, but I have. Maybe with this kind of training I could control the damage and keep out of trouble."

"What do you mean that you have hurt people?" Gary was a little concerned, he didn't need any extra problems on this trip.

"In my country things are very bad. It is very hard for those who want to obey the law. In the last ten years the pirates from my country have become rich ransoming the crews of big ships. They take whatever they want from the people, and aren't afraid of anything."

He was angry and his voice reflected it. "One day a couple of them came to our village and they started following some of the young girls, including my sister. When they tried to drag my sister behind a building, I killed them. I killed them both."

He looked Gary in the eyes again and said, "With this training I would only hurt them. Then I don't have to leave my home. My family doesn't take me away to America."

Gary realized the kid was homesick and didn't like being in the U.S.. He could see himself as a kid arguing with his father about having to move again to Cambodia, or France, or Russia. There was something about this kid Geedi that he liked, maybe he reminded him of himself at that age.

In the end there was nothing wrong with teaching the kid some of the basics. They had time on their hands anyways. Gary got Geedi to work on basic foot positioning, learning to create better balance. He kept pushing the boy in the shoulder, knocking him off balance until the kid got it right and started being able to fend off shoves from the bigger man.

Then Gary started moving around Geedi and pushing him from different positions that he wasn't expecting. The kid was again being pushed around until he figured out to keep balanced in any situation. He told Geedi to practice his balance exercises consistently, it was the most important thing he would learn.

Since they had some time to waste, he exposed the youngster to the concept of using an opponent's momentum against him. He had Geedi throw a punch at him and he stepped outside of the punch, got his balance, then grabbing the teen's wrist. At the same time he shifted his own weight in the direction the punch had been going and used Geedi's momentum to keep him moving right on past.

Then Gary took some slow punches at Geedi and let him get used to the idea of grabbing his opponent's wrist and keeping him going forward. The teen was quick to understand that the move was designed to keep the attacker off balance and that his own balance gave him the leverage to complete the move.

Eventually they heard a call from the cafeteria and stopped to eat. Gary noticed that Vanessa was placing a cloth of some sort over one of the tables. He didn't know where she had found it, but almost laughed when he saw her pull a small candle out of the shopping bag sized purse she carried.

When she realized that everyone was watching her, she stopped and looked at them wide-eyed, "What are you people all looking at?"

"Well Vanessa, it looks like that table is too small for all of us." Gary volunteered.

Vanessa stood straight up and placed her hands on her ample hips, "Of course not." Then she gave a big smile, rubbing her hands together as her hips seemed to almost wiggle, "This table is for me and Mike."

Everyone burst out laughing except Mike. He laid his head down on his arms pretending he wasn't part of the conversation. As Victor pushed Mike gently from behind, the laughing continued.

Gary pulled out the chair and adjusted it for Vanessa as she sat down. Mike was so conscious of his blushing that he didn't hear everyone as they clapped and cheered. Everyone laughed as Vanessa winked and blew kisses at her dinner partner until he couldn't hold back any longer and joined the circus. It was a moment of release that they all needed. Finally, everyone else settled down and they had some food.

*****

Later that evening Gary had Deuce and Victor move the trigger supplies into a small room. He didn't want to do this now, but had no choice. He was going to have to bring on the auras. It was all he could think of. They were pretty well right in Montréal and he still didn't know what to do. He really needed the auras to show him what the next step was.

Everyone had been relaxing for a while and he decided it was time to get going. "Okay guys, I have some bad news. We need some migraines."

No one was interested initially, none of them offered to get up and be first. "Come on everybody, we know this is the only way."

Chantal was starting to rise when Mary beat her to it. The old woman stood and announced. "I'm ready, let's start with the wine." It would have been funny if she didn't look so serious. Geedi stood next, and then the rest knew they were resigned to it and got up as well.

They all took a chair in the small room while Gary tried to explain his rationale, "I figure we try and get everyone at the same time. The problem will be coordinating the timing of the headaches."

No one had a problem with that, but Gary was concerned because if they couldn't get them at the same time it would mean going through a long process every time the auras were needed. In the back of his head he could just imagine what someone would think if they walked in on this bizarre setting.

The wine and chocolate made the rounds as he started the flashing light and turned up the ghetto blaster. Deuce stood to the side with Victor who had never seen one of these sessions, and couldn't seem to believe the scene in front of him.

Both Vanessa and Mary let him know they were feeling the throbbing starting. He had them hold still while they waited for the rest. As if on cue, Chantal raised her hand and Gary had three of them. He was worrying about the two men. He knew they would take longer and tried to speed it up.

He moved closer to Mike and Geedi who were sitting side by side and started yelling at them and shaking their chairs. He wanted to upset the apple cart a little more. He could tell that Vanessa and Mary were getting aggravated. Almost at the same time the two men motioned that they were feeling their headaches.

Gary jumped up and grabbed the light. He asked everyone to get up and stare at the map.

Chantal went first. "Gary there's no line in my vision at all." She sounded shocked.

"Nothing at all?"

"Nothing."

"I don't have a blank spot either." Mary never had a migraine without the spots. "I can't believe it."

"Well you better, because I don't see any either." Vanessa sounded delighted that they were gone. "Now if the headache would just go away with it."

Gary didn't expect that and was stumped again. Without the auras they were done. Was this the end? He still didn't know what to do. They couldn't be stopped now. They had just started.

Then Geedi spoke up. "I see the bar in my vision. I have my aura." He seemed pleased with himself.

"So do I, but it's different." Mike's voice was strained.

Gary was back in the game and wanted better explanations. "What is different? Describe it."

Mike took a second while he thought about it. "It's a smaller bar and I don't know why, but I don't think it fits on this map."

Gary had thought about other possibilities they might encounter when they got to Montréal and he'd made sure they had a local map.

Gary grabbed the map from the pile of supplies. Deuce helped him pin it up, and then they stood back to let Geedi and Mike look at it. The two of them agreed that the bar fit better on this map, but that they didn't know where to start from.

Gary had to think about that one. Back in the shelter he'd measured the distance from Chantal's spot to the wall.

Gary paced off the five steps. He moved a chair to mark the spot. "Okay, try standing right around here."

Mike and Geedi stood beside the chair and started moving slightly to each side and backwards and forwards trying to line up on something. Mike commented, "I'm still not sure but I think it's right there. Don't know what's there though."

Gary walked up to the map and pointed with his finger. "Direct me to the spot."

Mike and Geedi issued directions as Gary moved his finger until they yelled in unison, "Stop."

Mike continued. "Right there, that's the square end. Move slightly to your left and that's the point."

Gary stared closely at the map. Southwest of Montréal. They would have to go back across the river. He looked where the point of the bar was pointing and still didn't see much. "Make sure you're right on the line of the chair."

After the two men made slight adjustments the point seemed to be landing in Saint Hubert. This name meant something, but he couldn't remember what. "Chantal. What's in Saint Hubert?"

The three woman had been suffering their migraines for a while now and were clearly in some discomfort. Chantal didn't have an answer. To her there was nothing special there. "I don't know Gary. It's the same as any other friggin' place." She pushed her fingertips into her temples, "There's really nothing I can think of except that old Air Force Base there. I don't know."

A military connection was intriguing. Somewhere that made sense to him. He wasn't sure why, but if there was something really big about these messages and you were supposed to cross into different countries then who could keep something quiet and away from the public better than the military. Who could arrange things and was better equipped to handle it? Especially with the way the American and Canadian militaries worked together so much. It was going to be really interesting to get to the end of this and see exactly who and what was involved. Gary figured they had everything they were going to get from this session, and he needed to research this military base in Saint Hubert.

"Okay, everyone get your meds going. Thanks guys."

Everyone rushed out to get their pills and Gary used his cell phone to open up a hot spot and fired up his laptop.

The base had been closed down in ninety-seven, but the 438 tactical helicopter wing was still stationed there.

Something told Gary that this message thing wasn't new. He knew headaches had been around for ages, all the way back to early times. So he figured the message had been there a while. He looked farther back into the base's history and realized it was once the main station for the Royal Canadian Air Force Air Defence Command Headquarters.

This meant that the base was significant at one time. So there might be some reason this was their goal. Well, they would see in the morning.

*****

If spending Saturday night on meds had been fun for the team, then driving around Saint Hubert on Sunday morning wasn't a lot better. The two vans were approaching the area of town that had once been the military base and Gary knew that there would be security cameras around the airport that was still there.

If they didn't want to seem suspicious they were going to have to drive by no more than twice. Anything else would stand out and they didn't need that. There was a road around the perimeter of the airfield that went past the buildings and hangers. Gary planned to drive around the whole place.

He kept their speed down and slowly worked his way around the field and past the hangers. They were going past a group of unremarkable buildings when the van exploded.

"Ahhhhhh." Gary looked to see Chantal with her hands clamped over her ears.

"Shit, that hurts" Came just as quick from Geedi and then Vanessa started to yell, "Stop it!"

Gary looked in the rear view mirror and Mike was grimacing while Mary had her eyes closed tight, her face contorted in pain.

What was happening? Shit, he couldn't stop here because they'd stay in the pain. He had to keep moving and hope whatever it was stopped.

As they got farther from the buildings the problem went away, but not before Chantal ended up bent over in the seat and Vanessa had let out one of her screams. He didn't know what to think about what had just happened and headed back to the safety of the warehouse.

They had to leave the next morning, and he knew that they were already jacked up and aggravated, so there was no better time. "I know this will sound crazy, but I think we should look at the visions again."

Someone groaned, and another sighed. As Geedi rose from his chair, someone else cursed. Gary felt bad, but he couldn't see another choice as he led them to the small room. He wondered about what had happened at the base, he still didn't understand what they were supposed to do. The lights were flashing and the music pounding in the room vibrated in everyone's ears. After the trauma at the air force base it didn't take long. Chantal and the two women were getting quick migraines. "I see a line now Gary. It stands out clearly."

"I can see a blank spot again," came from Vanessa. "So do I" from Mary.

Gary checked Mike and Geedi and knew they were close. They always had this far off look as they became irritated. One, and then the other, nodded that they were getting going.

Gary turned back to the women. "Okay, how does it land on the map?"

Chantal was quick to answer, "It doesn't Gary. The line looks like it belongs on the big map."

Gary motioned Deuce to help him switch out the Montréal map for the North American one. He reminded Chantal to stand by the chair at the right distance.

Chantal held on to the back of the chair as she focused on the map. "The line seems wrong. It goes off the map up past Hudson Bay."

"What about you two?" Gary looked at Mary and Vanessa.

Vanessa said hers was the same as it had been before. It was to the west of Montréal. Mary added, "Mine is the same."

Gary had always wondered what the blank spots were for. So far they hadn't done anything. Now the blank spot was clearly to the west of Montréal. Maybe that was it. He had Deuce help him adjust the map again, giving it a quarter turn.

Gary looked back at her, "Well?"

She still couldn't believe this was really happening. The line fit perfectly. She struggled again with the fact that there really was a message in her head. "You won't believe me, it goes right across the county following the highways up into Alaska. I can't see the name," she trailed off.

Then she moved closer to the map, "It goes to Fairbanks, Alaska." And she set her finger over the name.

Mike stood beside Chantal, "It works for me, my bar is right at the tip of where she says her line goes. I vote for Fairbanks as well."

Geedi jumped off his chair and went over to see for himself. "He's right Gary. I see the same thing. It is pointing to that city."

"Okay, we're done. Everyone get out of here and take a break. You need to rest and I need to think." He motioned to the two big guys. "Deuce and Victor. You guys want to hang back for a minute."

Gary waited until they were alone and the others were gone. "This just became a long trip. What do you guys think? Are you up for it?"

Deuce didn't care where they went. He knew this trip was something special and he wanted to be there. "No problems here boss. I'm with ya."

Victor had made a quick call to Ivan. "We'll go till we finish. Then I go back to New York."

"Deal." Gary grinned at the big Russian.

CHAPTER 25

Both private jets were landing about the same time. They had flown under cover of darkness to land in small fields outside Montréal and Toronto. Alexi had decided he needed to stop these people before they solved the message and told any others.

Getting his men into Canada undetected was a little difficult, but late-night landings at remote fields had always worked for drug planes, and it would work for him.

Alexi made sure that the pilots were legit, and that they were going to do all the communicating on behalf of the group. The pilots would be the only ones who would enter any airport buildings, and speak to any officials. Everyone else would keep their heads down until a vehicle was brought alongside the plane.

He had made it clear to Turov, and the crews, that he wanted them watching all the major highways in and out of Montréal and Toronto. He had to split up his men until he found them again – if he found them again. Turov had a third crew, but didn't know where to send it. He would hold it back and use it when necessary. Each of the crew leaders had phone numbers for contacts on the north side of the border. They had to meet up with these contacts to secure vehicles and weapons. He didn't know where Alexi had gotten the numbers, or who was on the other end, but he didn't care either. He was more concerned with finding the targets.

It wasn't until the crews let him know they were set that he was satisfied and able to relax a bit. They were ready to go. He discussed possible routes in and out of each city with his crews.

The Toronto crew would be watching the 400-highway north out of the city, and both the 403 and 401 that went west out of Toronto. There was only the 401 going east. Four spots ensured they were watching the major routes.

Montréal had the 416 from Ottawa and the 401 from Toronto on the west side of the city. Highway 20 led to Quebec City on the east side. So they only needed to watch the three routes there. He told his leaders to make sure their crews got as much rest as they could that night, and that they were sharp and ready to go in the morning.

They had to hope that the targets were stopped in Montréal for a day or so, and they hadn't already made it out of the city. Getting his men on the ground that night was the quickest Turov could do.

*****

Ivan was restless, his brain had been working on this Septon problem non-stop. Now he had the man from Russia calling making demands. There had been a time years ago when Ivan had to answer daily to someone above him. He didn't like it.

He'd worked hard at creating insulation between himself and the top. He didn't like returning to answering to someone. Especially, when he didn't know who it was.

Since he had found the information his caller wanted, he took out his special cell phone. He was trying to understand the request and how the answer fit in. He couldn't. There was no sense delaying any longer, and he punched in the number.

The old voice answered, "Yes?"

"Its Ivan." he hesitated, "I have the information you asked for."

The old man sounded like he had a surge of energy. "Good. Tell me, what did you find?"

"We created a situation where this Alexi Tambov had to hand something to one of our people. He was missing the third finger on his right hand." There was a silence that he didn't understand, "Is that what you wanted?"

The silence persisted while Ivan waited. Again he heard excitement, and a note of relief in the voice. "You've done very well. I am in your debt. Now let me think."

He kept quiet, wondering what was coming next. He waited for the old man to come to some conclusion. The old man suddenly had questions. "Tell me everything you have uncovered about Tambov."

Ivan figured he had nothing to lose. "His money comes from off-shore, we traced it to Belize. This particular Tambov didn't exist before ninety-two, so it must be a fake name. He settled in the U.S. and started building the research facility five years ago. It's been up and running for a few years. I don't know much more."

"What is the facility for?"

This was a question that he didn't want. He had to be careful. Did this man already have the answer and was just testing him? If the Russian didn't know about the message, then Ivan didn't want to tell him. He saw the message as an opportunity and wasn't telling anyone if he could help it. This guy was dangerous.

Ivan decided to take the gamble, "It says they do research to help people with brain issues and to help develop medications. I'm not really sure though."

The silence that followed was frightening. He was waiting to see if he'd just hung himself. The old man's next words made him feel he was still okay. "You did good. I'll be in touch."

Ivan stuck the phone back in his pocket. He realized he was tense, and sat back, letting out a long slow breath. He felt his spine relax as he took a few more deep breaths to finally get his heart rate down. He was having a hard time reading that old man and Ivan knew that was a problem.

*****

The team packed up and left Montréal in the middle of the night.

Gary had wanted to start out in the dark. He figured the border would only stop Septon for so long. The farther they got from Montréal the better.

Alaska. He couldn't believe that was where they were going. It was somewhere he'd always said he wanted to go. Gary decided they wouldn't take the fastest route, which was to follow the TransCanada highway through northern Ontario and across the prairies.

The route through Toronto to Sarnia, and across back into Michigan where they could follow the border along the U.S. side, would be better for the group. Being in their own country would reduce their anxiety. He figured they'd hit Toronto just after rush hour.

At five o'clock they were crawling through westbound traffic and they hadn't even made it into Toronto yet. It was obviously going to take some time. When they cleared the other side of the city two hours later, Gary was relieved. From here it was clear sailing straight to the U.S. border. They would avoid the Windsor-Detroit crossing by sticking to the smaller Sarnia-Port Hope route. From there it was a short run through Flint and Lansing, to Chicago.

$$*****$$

From his vantage point on the overpass, Septon's soldier had watched the truck roll down the 401 into Toronto. He'd placed the call and been picked up. Next they had to wait to hear which way the targets exited the city. Two hours later the call came, the rental vans were seen leaving the city, still on the 401, heading west.

Petrov had too many vehicles spread out over the city. He got his crew together in a pair of SUV's and they took off in pursuit of the rentals. He wasn't going to miss another opportunity. Not a second time.

They couldn't make up any distance until the traffic cleared out past the suburbs. With the pedal pinned to the floor the SUV was moving fast to catch up. An hour later they had the rentals in their sights. The crew leader called Turov with an update, and was given specific instructions.

"Do it on the highway. Motorists will be flying by too fast to focus on what's happening. You can use the guardrails on that road to keep them penned in. Do it quick."

Petrov just had to decide where. He realized there wouldn't be a perfect spot, he would have to force the situation.

$$*****$$

Deuce had been keeping a close eye on the traffic around him, and was the first to notice the two SUV's flying up behind them.

"Do you see those two black SUVs coming up fast behind us?"

The big Russian started watching them out his side mirror. "Yeah, got 'em."

"They're running pretty tight together. Might mean business."

"I think you're right. It also looks like a number of people in those vehicles."

"Hand me my phone." Deuce thumbed quick-dial, "We got company. Two fully-loaded black SUVs."

"Shit. What do you want to do?" Gary knew that Deuce and Victor were the men he had to rely on for this stuff.

Victor reached over to take the phone. "Get off at the next exit, wait to make your move until the very last second. We will make sure they miss the exit. We'll reconnect after we get rid of them."

Instead of getting into a fight, Victor wanted them out of the picture all together. That made sense to Gary. No sense taking any chances with the cargo. "Okay, we'll take the one coming up now."

Everyone in the front van was alarmed by the call. They looked out the back of the van, trying to spot their tail. Except Mary, she sat with her hands folded on her lap, staring straight out the front windshield. Gary slowed just slightly. He knew he had to take the ramp as fast as he could, but he didn't want to roll the thing.

"They've seen us," the soldier in the front of the SUV lowered his binoculars. "They're all looking back out the window."

Petrov knew he had to act now. He had really wanted the element of surprise on his side, now he would have to settle for using force. He accelerated towards the second van. The other SUV had instructions to stay with him and be there when he tried to stop the front vehicle.

Deuce slowly moved over and covered half of the lane, just as the SUV pulled out to pass. He didn't want to move over any more, because he was afraid the second SUV might pass him on the other side.

In the mirror Gary watched Deuce move across the lane and block the SUV's.

He was wondering what the guys were going to do, but had to forget them and concentrate on the exit ramp that was quickly going by. He gripped the steering wheel hard. Deuce eased back into his own lane as he anticipated the SUVs surging past.

Gary swung the truck sideways at the last second, aiming towards the last few feet of ramp. The van rocked and the tires fought to maintain their grip as he strong-armed the vehicle in the new direction and slid onto the off-ramp.

Petrov realized what had just happened. "Brake. Brake. Get over. Don't let them escape!"

Deuce anticipated their next move, slowing alongside the SUVs. They wanted over and Deuce only had to hold them a second longer. Now they were past the exit, and Deuce knew Gary was gone. He stepped on the accelerator and moved ahead of the two SUVs.

The crew leader was livid. Fuck. He'd missed them again. He couldn't turn back on the major highway and backing up along the roadside wouldn't help, the first van was long gone.

"Stay with the second van. I want those guys."

The SUVs flew down the road, racing to catch up to the van. Deuce was hoping they would follow. He was sure Victor could handle himself. He always wanted a piece of these guys. "Okay, we have nobody to protect now. What do you say we take it to these assholes?"

"Turn off at the next exit. Find a mall." Victor's deep voice sounded serious, but he was smiling widely. He reached down into one of his bags and pulled out the weapon he'd gotten from their contact in Montréal. He slid the mag out and confirmed it was full. He looked over at Deuce. "This'll be fun."

Deuce hadn't necessarily been thinking about killing anybody. He'd been thinking messing them up, but Victor was right. Any discussion they engaged in should have a degree of finality to it. The next off-ramp was coming fast and Deuce slowed just enough to make the corner. He hung on tight, hoping the tires didn't let go as they whipped around the long curve.

"Keep them thinking that you are afraid and trying to get away," Victor told him.

Deuce didn't slow down for the red light at the end of the ramp. Looking both ways before he got there, he threw the van around the corner, and headed southbound. The two SUVs had both struggled to make the ramp and didn't slow for the red light either. The second SUV almost T-boned a car as it flew through the light and slid sideways, bouncing off the metal guardrail back onto the road.

Deuce wove in and out of traffic, looking for a mall. The big Wal-Mart sign caught his attention first and he aimed for it. A block later he turned into the parking lot.

"Go right through the parking lot, around to the back." Victor instructed.

Deuce went around the side of the building with the SUVs following, towards the truck loading docks.

"Drop me soon as you're around the last corner," said Victor. "Keep going thirty meters and then stop and wait. Be ready."

Deuce slowed quickly to drop off Victor after they rounded the corner, then stepped on it. When he got far enough away, he stopped and waited, the transmission in gear.

Petrov started to get a bad feeling about following the van behind the mall. What were they doing? The only reason to go back there would be to get out of the way. By the time he realized that this would be a good place to ambush someone, it was too late, the SUV was already rounding the corner.

He looked at the parked van idling quietly, its brake lights glowing and ordered his driver to stop. The second SUV came around the corner and stopped behind them. Petrov was turning to order his driver to get them out of there when he saw a figure step out of the shadows with a gun raised at shoulder level.

Victor calmly fired through the side window at the driver. Two shots, although he was sure the first shot hit when the driver's head exploded in a mass of red. Now crouched down beside the SUV, he leaned out to find the driver of the second vehicle. With his arm already raised, he sighted on the front windshield and let off two more rounds.

One of the two bullets would find its target. The driver slammed back against the seat as his face blew open. Victor took a second to lean out even further and blow out the front tires of the second SUV.

He looked down and put a couple rounds into the tires of the first SUV as well. With the two vehicles out of commission he started running for Deuce, counting on shock and confusion to give him the couple extra seconds he needed.

Petrov ducked when the first shots went off. He'd felt his driver's warm blood as it sprayed across his face, bits of bone and grey matter oozing into his hair. He'd heard the second shot, but was surprised when he didn't feel an impact. Quickly, he tried to get his hands into his pack resting on the floor between his feet.

The exploding sound of the tires on the second van being shot out were clear. Petrov's hand found the gun in the pack at the same time he felt his own van rock as the two wheels on the drivers side were shot out. He knew he needed to react. Jesus. He caught a glimpse of a big guy running to the van in front as he levered open his passenger side door.

By the time Petrov had gotten out from behind the door of the SUV, the subject's van was accelerating away. Dammit. They'd been surprised and caught flat-footed. He was in trouble now with Turov. How was he was going to explain two dead soldiers and both target vehicles gone. He'd lost them.

CHAPTER 26

The situation was changing. Gary was the one with information now. The fact that they'd gotten away again was lucky. The fact that Deuce and Victor made Septon pay a price was just part of this journey.

He wasn't too worried about attracting police attention, he was sure Septon's men would have cleaned up anything that would bring attention to them. He and Deuce had returned the rental vehicles and the whole team was holed up in a hotel with hot food and hot showers. They shouldn't be found for a while.

The fact that Gary had figured out how to read the messages gave him the advantage. He knew where he was going. Alaska was going to be a long drive. Flying was a good idea, but arriving at an airport without supplies or ground transport wasn't.

After some time on his laptop, he left the team in the hotel and caught a cab outside the front lobby. Everyone was tired enough to find their separate spaces and kick back to relax.

Victor was cleaning his gun in the room he shared with Deuce. If Deuce had any reservations about Victor, they were gone now. The guy was seriously deadly, which was just fine with him. He was sure that this would get uglier before they got wherever they were going. Alaska, Christ, he couldn't believe it.

Mike was sitting on the couch in Vanessa and Mary's room The woman was fussing over him again, getting as close as she could, touching him, patting his arm, trying to hold his hand. Chantal noticed that Mike was getting embarrassed. She looked at Mary, and with a nod of her head towards the door mimicked taking a drag on a cigarette.

Mary just nodded.

The two women stood outside the front lobby quietly smoking their cigarettes.

"Do you wonder what's going to be at the end?" Mary asked.

"You know, not really." Chantal thought a second, "I should be though. It's been like a nightmare since this whole thing started, and all I was thinking about was getting back to my normal life."

"I don't know girl, something like this might be so big you never get your old life back."

Chantal was left with a new set of things to think about. Mary was right. What was at the end of this whole thing? And what did it mean to her and Gary, or the rest of them for that matter. What would it mean to solve this crazy message?

The taxi dropped Gary off at Marken Performance, in the old section of Waterloo. He was looking for an out of the way garage that had some skilled racecar techs.

His biggest problem was that time was critical.

The couple old beauties parked outside were a good sign. A jacked-up old bronco rag-top hitched to a trailer weighted down with a seventy-seven Camaro with a big-assed supercharger sticking out the hood made him think he was in the right place. Through the open garage doors he could see a Mustang on one side and an old white Galaxy on the other. Someone noticed him standing at the door. The guy lifting his head out of the Galaxy started cleaning his hands on a rag while he headed towards Gary.

"Mark," the mechanic stuck out his hand. "Can I help you?"

"I sure hope so." He needed this guy to understand how critical their situation was, without giving up too much detail.

"The thing is, I need two trucks right now. Cost isn't my issue, time is. Check me out if you want. I'm in a bad position, and need something special that I can rely on."

Mark had questions before committing to anything. Gary had a number of things he rattled off while the mechanic made notes. Finally they shook hands and Gary left the shop.

*****

The team crossed back into the U.S. at Port Hope as planned, and headed west across the country. With Deuce and Victor switching off in the second vehicle and Gary, Chantal and Mike taking turns up front, they were making pretty good mileage. A stopover in Chicago let them sleep, shower and get a hot meal that didn't come through a drive-thru window.

They stuck to I-90 until they hit Montana and had to head north into Alberta. Then they crossed British Columbia and the Yukon, finally hitting the Alaska border four hundred and seventy-five miles short of Fairbanks.

The guys at Marken had done a great job. Their connections had come up with a fairly new Hummer that had been upgraded in a few key areas, and a four-door Dodge pickup with a big Cummings diesel motor. Both vehicles had obviously had some pretty serious engine upgrades and had the right stuff to off-road if necessary. The fuel consumption was the only issue Gary could see.

As they had all settled into the road trip, the team had grown closer. Victor sometimes joined Chantal and Mary on their smoke breaks. Chantal liked the old woman's wit and sarcasm. She told Gary she wondered what Mary had been like when she was younger. He didn't wonder at all. They were spitting images of each other.

Vanessa and Mike were engaged in an ongoing skirmish. Vanessa flirted, while Mike fought a losing battle of pretending he didn't care. The two would squirrel away together in the back seat while Chantal and Mary shook their heads at the noise.

They'd had a trigger session along the way to make sure they were still on track and everything was still pointing to Fairbanks. Gary hoped it was the end of the travelling. This was a long way to go for just another waypoint where they received more directions. He hated to think it, but he was pretty sure there was more to come.

At least he was comfortable he could read the signs now. Chantal was the main line. The extra bars were for finding the specific spot once they arrived. The blank spots told Chantal which way her line was to be aimed for the next location.

The fact that the blank spot was now lining up south of Fairbanks made him think that they would be going somewhere else, but right now all that mattered was Alaska. They drove through the Yukon and were finally back in the U.S. again, roaring up highway two, towards Fairbanks. Eight more hours.

*****

Turov sat nervously across from Alexi. His men had missed both their opportunities, and now they had lost the targets completely. He didn't need his boss to say anything to know that the man was pissed. The paperweight that had been sitting on the wide desk had just smashed off the wall as Alexi shook visibly. Turov was trying hard to think of answers to questions that hadn't been asked yet. He would do whatever he needed to do to keep himself on Alexi's good side.

"Why have you let me down like this?" Alexi roared.

"We are trying to not bring attention to ourselves and these targets know that. They have been on public roads and in public places since this started." He cleared his throat and continued, "I personally will be leading the next attempt. We have crews standing by to be flown out as soon as we have a location."

"Yes. When, you have a location." Turov picked up on the slight change in Alexi's voice. "I'm curious. How long should I give you to find a new location?"

He was clear on the meaning seeping out between the lines. *Remember what happened to Sergi.* "We've found them each time so far, and we will get another chance at them."

"You'd better."

Alexi dismissed the man and leaned back in his chair. This Gary Collins was living up to his reputation. He smashed his fist down on the table, he couldn't believe someone was trying to beat him to this thing he'd been after all his life.

Turov was packed and ready to move, he just needed some luck. He had his teams spread out across the country. Mainly they were watching major highways, but Turov had other contacts he could tap into for extra sets of eyes. He'd posted on message boards that catered to the criminal element, and told everyone what he was looking for. Now he just needed one break.

CHAPTER 27

The team had been quiet for hours. Everyone just stared out at the endless rolling wilderness that was Alaska. Idly, Gary wondered how much unused land there was up here. *Why was anyone even up here in the first place?*

Now the sun was down it was dark, and remote as hell outside. When they arrived at the small group of lights that represented Fairbanks, Gary knew they all needed a break. He pulled up to the first hotel he found.

He wasn't staying any longer than he had to. This place was too small to hide in and Septon would find them easily if they had anyone watching.

Everyone got their rooms sorted out, grabbed some food and were back in the hotel. Chantal was just starting to relax when she noticed Gary standing patiently by the door.

"What's up? You look like you're waiting for something."

"I'm waiting for the right time. Everyone is already tired and stressed. It's the perfect time to get the headaches going and find out what's going on."

"God. Can't this wait until morning? Everyone could use some rest."

"Look, if we do them tonight I can make plans overnight and we can be ready to go first thing, instead of later in the day. We want to get out of this town before Septon catches up."

Geedi was up first. He'd been spending all his spare time with either Gary, or Victor and Deuce. He wanted to impress Gary and was just waiting for another chance to do some more training. "I'm okay to do it."

Mike freed himself from Vanessa's adventurous hands and joined Geedi, "I'm okay too."

He held Chantal's gaze and shrugged his shoulders as if to say, *well?*

"Jesus, Gary, I've been on meds for a couple weeks straight now. I've had more damned migraines in the last month than in the past six months. This is crazy." She was getting up though, and he knew that Mary would join her. Suddenly, everyone was staring at Vanessa.

She'd had enough migraines herself lately, but she was never one to hold people back, she was usually the leader of her group of friends back home. "Aw, hell."

Gary nodded to Deuce, and he and Victor went to set up the trigger supplies in their room. Gary didn't even put up the North American map. He knew they would need a local one, and anticipating that, had picked up a Fairbanks map when they stopped for gas.

Just like in Montréal, Chantal didn't see her line and the two other women didn't see their blank spots. Both Geedi and Mike had bars pointing to somewhere north of Fairbanks. Gary got up close to the map and didn't see anything at the spot, just a paved road going that direction with branches heading off into the wilderness. *What could possibly be out there?*

He knew there was a lot of mining and gas exploration up here. He had the guys try moving slightly and made sure they were the right distance from the map. Their indicators kept landing in the middle of nowhere, to the west of the main road.

This was a new problem. He wasn't worried about trying to drive into the backcountry with the trucks they had. Both the Hummer and Dodge would handle almost anything just fine, providing they didn't get into any real trouble or real bad terrain. But if they ran into Septon they would have a big problem out in the middle of nowhere.

He looked at the natural lay of the land, trying to pick out some landmarks near where the bars were landing on the map. He'd need to find that spot with what little information he was getting here. The spot was about one hundred miles north of Fairbanks just past a series of three lakes west of the road, so it should be easy to find.

He had a feeling that things were going to get worse all of a sudden. He wanted to spend some time with Chantal.

CHAPTER 28

Turov needed to get in front of things. He'd offered up money on the right channels and was sure there were people watching. A group in Montréal who wanted to keep quiet had information for sale. It never failed to amaze him what money could buy, including disloyalty.

Ivan's contacts in Montréal had not only provided a safe house, but had shadowed them the whole time they were in the province. Now they had no problem offering that information up for the right price. The target's vans had been seen near a military base south of Montréal. Alexi had been excited to know there might be a military connection.

Turov had a couple of men on the phones following up leads nonstop since the chase began. The first call came in two days ago from a trucker who spotted two vehicles with Ontario plates and a bunch of people in them driving through Montana. Could be anybody, but the truck descriptions were good to have. A dark blue Hummer and a red Dodge pickup.

The second call sent Septon into action. A gas station owner called in to the number on the website, sure he had the vehicles in question. He identified a blue Hummer with a tall white male driver and five passengers. The second vehicle was a red Dodge with a black driver and a really big white passenger.

Turov needed to fly to Toronto to pick up both the Montréal and Toronto crews before heading to Fairbanks. This was his chance to make things right.

Alexi had made the call, he wanted them stopped. He couldn't take the chance that they got to the end before he did. He would allow Turov to follow them to the end as a last resort, but would rather stop them before they got there. Alexi was confident that now that he knew there was really a message and he just needed to bring a couple of them back here and get the answers out of them.

The isolation up in Alaska was just what they needed. They would have some room to work and the targets would be limited in where they could go. Alexi had them cornered, and was sure that once Turov arrived he would get things under control. Now all they had to do was get there before the targets moved on.

*****

The team had resupplied, purchased some spare gas cans, and made sure they had extra of everything before they headed north out of Fairbanks. Gary knew they were on their own once they hit the dirt roads. If they broke down and someone happened to come along that would be great, but the chances of someone coming by if they were stranded on a side road was bleak at best.

The distance out to their destination, together with the speeds they would be able to travel on these roads, meant they were probably going to be spending the night out there and coming back in the morning.

An hour after they turned off the highway they were slowly working their way through ruts and potholes when they passed the first vehicle. The mining truck lumbered on past without slowing down.

They were all being jolted around inside the Hummer as the suspension worked overtime to smooth out the road. Gary noticed the odd side road with a sign listing a mine and the name of the company that built it.

The mostly treeless hills allowed them to see for miles when they topped a knoll. Unfortunately, other than the scenery, there was nothing to see. Finally Gary came to a stop. This was the final turn-off to the lakes, this was where they were on their own.

Resigned to seeing it through, he turned the wheels and started up the side road. The going was slower, and it became apparent he had to pay attention to the ruts and washouts when he saw the first four-foot drops into one of them. You wouldn't want to be doing this at night. Any one of these holes would swallow up a truck and unless you had a winch, you'd be staying there. Some of the holes needed to be avoided entirely because they were full of water.

As the afternoon was getting late Gary stopped on top of a hill where they had a good sightline. He hoped to see the lakes they were searching for. They had to be in the right area now.

Everyone piled out of the trucks for a chance to stretch their legs or gaff down a cigarette. He didn't ask how everyone was. He was thrilled they'd gotten this far without complaints.

Deuce joined him up in front of the trucks, looking out over the endless landscape. "I'm wondering where our friends are."

Gary was too. He hoped that they'd lost them coming across the country and that they wouldn't see them again, but knew that was unlikely. "Just keep your eyes open and be ready."

The two men continued to stare out over the valley and Gary pointed out the lakes he was looking for, "I think we need to find another side road down there by the lakes."

"Gary, you see that reflection over more to the left?" Deuce pointed.

Gary tracked his view to the left and didn't stare but just kept his gaze general. The flash was there, he caught it once then twice. Now that he had a location he zoomed in and tried to identify what they were seeing. He couldn't figure it out. Well, they were going to find out soon enough. He turned to the team and called, "All right you guys, break's over."

As the two trucks rumbled down into the valley Gary kept trying to get a look at whatever was causing the reflection. They were almost at the lakes when he figured out that it was light was reflecting off the metal panels that had been used to roof an old cabin.

The terrain that had been dry up on the hilltop became muddier and sloppier to drive in near the bottom. He stopped in the middle of the road. It wasn't like anyone else would be coming along. He told Chantal and the team he wanted to check out the cabin.

Victor climbed out of the Dodge to follow, but Gary wouldn't have it. He didn't say so to Victor, but he didn't want to scare anybody who might be there. Just seeing Victor walking around might be enough for some people. Besides, if Victor was there and something got a little tense he might pull a gun, and that wasn't what Gary needed here. He just needed information.

At the end of the road were an old cabin and a couple of outbuildings. They hadn't seen them at first because the buildings and their roofs were made all of wood. He was taken aback by all the stuff cluttered around the place. He was busy looking at all the snow machines, four wheelers, a few old trucks, a bulldozer, and scrap metal piles everywhere when he noticed the dogs.

They looked like sled dogs, a mix of malamutes and huskies strung out on chains that created a fence around the property. Gary slowed his walk almost to a stop. Once he got a little closer to the dogs and noticed they were watching him intently, he stopped completely.

"Hello! Is there anyone around?" he called.

"Who's asking?" The gruff voice sounded a little on the older side.

Gary started to turn towards the voice, but before he could answer it spoke again.

"Freeze. Don't move an inch. Don't turn this way or I'll shoot you. Sure as shit."

Gary froze. He didn't know the etiquette out here, but figured it pretty well included doing whatever the man with the gun said.

"Hi there. No harm meant. Gary Collins is the name." He spread his arms away from his sides, hands raised slightly.

"What'd'ya want?"

"I was just going to ask some questions about the area. We're on a trip and trying to find someplace."

"There aren't no places up here to find son. Just mines and wildlife. How many with ya in the trucks?"

Gary realized the old guy was on top of things. The fact he knew they had two trucks meant he'd been watching them come along the road, and had got himself in position to out-maneuver whoever came up his lane.

"There are eight of us. Three women, a kid, and three men."

"They call me Buck." The old man walked past Gary motioning him to follow. From the voice, he'd assumed the old man was white and wasn't ready to see the long black pony tail hanging down the back of his buckskin jacket. He could see the old man was still fit and strong. He had to be, living out here. The rifle in his hand reminded Gary again that this was no-man's land.

They approached the line of dogs chained to posts about fifteen feet apart. It looked like they were able to just reach each other at the ends of their chains. Gary felt a shiver thinking about stumbling on this place by mistake.

The dogs became aggressive as the two approached. He hung back a bit as they seemed to be looking past the old man, right at him.

"Easy boys, everything's fine."

This had an immediate effect and the dogs relaxed noticeably. Gary continued between the two nearest dogs, keeping an eye on them until he was out of chain range.

The old man pointed to a chair on the front deck and headed into the cabin. Looking at the overhang of the roof Gary wondered how safe it was sitting under it in the shade. The old man came out with the rifle still in his hand and leaned it against the wall as he sat down.

"You got questions. I got some of my own." The old man stared at Gary.

That was fair enough, "No problem. Fire away."

Buck sat there for a long time before he asked, "You the leader?"

"I don't think so," but they both heard the hesitancy in his voice.

"Sure you are. There's always been a leader."

What was he saying? Gary was stunned. Did the old man know why they were here? Had others been here looking for the message? Gary wanted to be straight with the old man.

"This trip just kind of happened. My girlfriend is involved and so I got involved. I tend to end up in charge of things, but I'm really not a leader, more like the organizer."

They sat quietly for another quarter hour until the old man turned to Gary. "You better tell that guy to go back to the trucks. If he gets too close to the dogs he's gonna have some trouble."

Gary was confused. He didn't know what Buck was talking about., "Pardon?"

"Your man out there. He's trying to sneak up on us, but the dogs have been watching him for a while now. He ain't fooling nobody."

Gary tried to see what the old man was watching. Then he noticed the dogs were all looking towards the south side of the property. Gary kept watching the dogs and could see that they were slowly turning their heads to the right as they tracked the scent and sound of someone moving out there.

He realized the old man could tell exactly where any intruder was. Good system.

"Victor, everything is fine, go back to the truck. I'll be there shortly," he stood on the deck and called out to the soldier.

Sure enough, the two men watched the dogs as their heads reversed themselves, rotating slowly to the left as Victor snuck back to the trucks.

"Where are you coming from?" Buck asked.

"We started in New York and went to Montréal before ending up here."

The old man was quiet again and Gary waited him out. He was trying to process the fact that others had come following the directions. What had they found here? What did the old man know?

"Well, you're lucky in one way and not in another," The old man said. "You'll find what you're looking for. I think you know it's down on the side-road by the lakes. But your answer ain't there, because all the others left here to go somewhere else. You seem to be on the right track, cause you did make it this far. And I can tell you that you'll be happier when you leave than when you arrived."

"What's down there by the lakes?'

There was more silence. Finally, without looking directly at him, Buck replied, "This journey is for you and your group, you'll find out shortly."

Obviously, he wasn't going to get an answer. Gary tried to ease things a bit, "Oh it can't be anything bad, probably just some wild sights to see."

"Well, take my warning for what it's worth. Every group that lands up here has always had another bunch following. It always works that way, and the second outfit is always a worse lot than the first."

Gary was pretty sure what he meant as he thought of Septon, but asked anyways, "What do you mean?"

"The first group is always like you, confused, out of place and on some aimless mission. The second group is usually all soldiers with a very specific goal. Killing off the first group."

"You've seen this?"

"I've seen them try and succeed in some cases. In others, I've seen battles and the first group escapes."

"You're crazy to stay out here where this kind of stuff is happening."

"Hey son, it's my land and the only thing crazy would be someone trying to come and bother me here. I got too many ways to cause you harm. Some of them found that out the hard way. No doubt some will learn it in the future as well."

Gary figured the old man had no plans on leaving any time soon. "People don't come every week, but they are starting to show up more'n once or twice a year now. Last group was eight months ago."

What was he supposed to say to that? He had no idea who was coming, but could make a good guess at why. Anyone could have solved the puzzle ahead of them. But if so, why hadn't they heard anything about it? Hadn't anyone made it to the end yet?

"How many teams like mine have you seen in your time up here?"

"Came here in the early eighties. It's been forty years, or so, I'd say. Must of seen forty to fifty groups in that time." Gary watched Buck rise and stretch. In the afternoon light it was apparent the man was a native. "You better get your people to come in here for the night. There's room and it's getting kinda late to venture around the lakes with the state of the road."

The idea of being safe from anything inside the ring of dogs was appealing. But he was worried about the others. Would they like being inside this old man's cabin for the night? "I'm not sure Buck."

"Suit yourself son. Thought you might need a place to do that crazy stuff with the lights and sounds like the others did."

Gary had to laugh. He wondered how much this old man had pieced together over the years. On some level he wondered how much he should believe of what the man said. Was he part of the whole process, or just watching it unfold? Either way, he was right that if they needed a place this would be a good one. Obviously the old man had watched other trying to bring on the visions.

"Thanks for the offer, but I think we'll head to the lakes tonight and camp down there so we can get out early tomorrow."

"Suit yourself son." The old man nodded. Then as he began walking away he gave Gary some help, "Look for the old government mine on the back side of the big lake."

They drove the Hummer down to the little track going around the lakes. It was in a lot worse shape than the other roads they'd been on so far. Gary was going side-to-side, around ruts and holes, more than he went straight.

He kept pushing forward around hills and over knolls, while watching to make sure the Dodge was keeping up. He thought they should be able to get around to the back of the lake and reach the mine site before it was too dark. That way they would be there tonight and could use the triggers before everyone turned in.

In some places there was no going around, he cautiously eased the front end of the Hummer into the muddy water, letting it sink until he hit bottom. Then keeping the engine revving, he pushed his way through the hole in low gear, praying the thing crawled out the other side. Deuce had a harder time with the Dodge and Gary could see the truck go up and then back a few times before crawling out of the bigger holes.

Finally they reached a rusted old signpost where he could just make out the government signage, and they turned onto a somewhat flatter road. They followed it around a hill and came to a stop by a pair of old buildings flanking a cave entrance.

The sun was close to setting and Gary was in a hurry. As soon as everyone was out of the trucks he insisted that they check out the place.

"Come on guys, let's see what's here."

Geedi didn't need encouragement, he ran off towards one of the buildings checking it out. Vanessa stepped out of the Hummer and groaned. This wasn't the kind excitement she had hoped for when jumping in to participate in this trip. If it weren't for Mike, she'd be freaking out by now.

Deuce and Victor spread out to have their own look around. Chantal and Mary were happy to get out of the damned truck and light up. Chantal couldn't believe that Mary was even standing after that ride.

Gary headed to the buildings to join Geedi. "Are they okay to sleep in tonight?"

"Yeah, roofs look good and it's dry inside."

Gary turned to everyone, "Hey, everyone put your stuff in this one here." He pointed to the bigger building. He returned to the truck to get his own stuff and everyone grabbed some part of their gear. Inside the building it was dusty and cobwebbed, but dry and open. Everyone dropped their stuff in various corners of the room.

"I say we check out the mine. It's dark, but we know the entrance is right here. We need to see what happens."

Geedi stepped forward as usual, but when no one else did Gary knew they were getting tired of it all. "Look, the old man confirmed this all means something. He doesn't know what, but he's watched people like us, in groups, coming here to find the message for forty years."

Gary let that sink in before he continued, "Honestly, I don't know what to think. It could be a hoax, or wild goose chase, but such a complex thing laid out like this speaks to something interesting."

"This has been going on for forty years?" Chantal was surprised.

"I really believe the old man when he said that we would be happier when we left than when we came. I think we're getting close to the end."

"Okay, Gary let's go. Anyone doesn't want to, they don't have to. Is that a deal?" She knew him too well, he'd just keep pushing until they all went along.

"Sure, that's fine with me." He figured enough of them would probably agree.

Gary reached for Chantal's hand and they joined Geedi by the door. Deuce and Victor were up instantly. The rest looked at each other and realized they'd come this far. They all headed out the door.

The old gate and warning signs sealed off the mouth of the mine. Victor and Deuce made quick work of them. Gary turned on the flashlight he'd grabbed as he stepped further inside.

He was glad when Chantal said to stop. He had hoped it wouldn't take long. He knew this was just a step, and the sooner they were done the sooner they moved forward. "What's wrong?"

"There's a slight pain and it's getting worse with each step. It's like in Montréal."

"I feel it now too." Vanessa backed up a few steps.

Gary looked at Mary and she nodded. Mike and Geedi stepped further into the mine and they both stopped suddenly. Geedi raised his hand to his forehead before stepping back. "Gary, I feel it too." Geedi and Mike both walked back to the group.

"We're out of here. That's all we need." He wanted them out as quickly as possible. He felt guilty as hell, his reason for leading them back to the building was not to let them rest, but to give them headaches. When they were all slumped on the floor of the building looking worse for wear, Gary jumped right in, "Okay, all we have left to do is line up the visions and we're through for the night."

Gary knew just by Chantal's look that she was pissed.

"Not a chance. That's it for me for tonight."

"You don't want to start tomorrow with a headache session do you? Does anyone? It's better now and then you can take your pills and sleep, and we just drive tomorrow."

They all knew it was the most logical thing to do, and they all grudgingly came around. Mary was first, "Okay dammit, let's get it done."

Gary noticed she was losing a little of her spunk, and hoped this was the last step for her sake.

Everyone else agreed, and Gary sent Deuce and Victor to get the supplies. It was definitely getting easier to start the migraines. The daily stress of the journey was piling up.

The message was there again, just as clear as the other times. The blank spot was south, so Gary turned the map upside down. Chantal lined up starting in Fairbanks, watching as her line stretched south through British Columbia and out of Canada into the U.S. again. It seemed to settle in northern Arizona.

The two guys had bars that pointed to a spot near the same place. It had been so hard to figure out in the beginning, and now that he understood the tools, it was easy to follow. They just had to get to Arizona and fine-tune the final location.

Why had the others before him been happy to leave here? Other than the isolation and potential dangers, he wondered if they had the same feeling he did that this was the end.

"Everyone eat something and get lots of sleep tonight if you can." Everyone was ignoring him at this point and Gary was starting to feel like the bad guy.

Outside he ran into both Victor and Deuce out patrolling. He told them both to pack it in, they shouldn't have any issues tonight. An hour later, refreshed by the clear night he made it back inside to find Chantal already wrapped up, asleep in her blankets. Gary got under the covers with her, wrapped his arms around her and pulled the blankets tight. He hoped she could hold out just a little longer.

CHAPTER 29

Turov stood there in the dark deciding what to do. They'd made it to Fairbanks and met up with the gas station owner who had ID'd the target's trucks as they came into the city.

Once he had sorted his crews into a couple of rentals, he'd met with their contact who'd followed the Hummer and Dodge north, returning once he knew which one of the side roads they'd turned off on. He told them these side roads always ended up at a mine or hunting camp and that Turov's crew should find whoever was down there at the end of the road.

Turov handed over a wad of cash and told him to keep watch until they returned.

They made good time until they hit the side road. Driving the rutted dirt road in the dark had been brutal. They'd pushed or pulled both vehicles a couple times. Going over the other side of a large hill they spotted moonlight reflecting dimly off something. Getting out the truck, he could hardly see anything through the night scope, but thought it might be a cabin with metal on the roof. It looked like the perfect spot for the targets to hole up.

Turov wasn't sure if he should hit them now, or wait for the morning. His men were trained and the targets weren't. His best opportunity was under the cover of darkness. He knew that there were a few soldiers down there, but that was offset by a bunch of women that they needed to protect.

If they'd already been heard he'd be running into a trap. Even so, it would be better to run into anything at night where his men's numerical superiority and combat skills would overwhelm the targets.

Finally, he decided it was time. He ordered two of his men to recon the place. One of them would come from behind and the other was to go in from the front. Three more would hold back just outside the perimeter, ready to come in once the recon turned up the best route.

Standing there in the dark, waiting to hear back from his patrol, the adrenaline was beginning to pump and the anticipation of battle was starting to get them all on edge. Turov was patient, but he was this close to pleasing Alexi, and could taste victory.

*****

The old man in the cabin was wide awake and dressed in his coat and boots. He never heard the sound of the planes that flew over regularly, but the slightest movement of the chains would wake him every time. Forty years of living in the wild and he'd become pretty dependant on them. From grizzlies to wolf packs, he'd seen it all.

Once the dogs woke him, he could get a rifle and take over. He'd shoot the bear, or a wolf or two if he could, but usually just a few shots in the air would chase off most of the trouble.

Tonight was different. He'd heard a truck running briefly when he'd woken and then it had shut off. Buck shook his head.

It looked like the followers had arrived. It amazed him how it happened every time, but none the less, here they were.

Experience said they would be criminals or soldiers, but it didn't matter; they'd have no manners and be ready to kill for the same information that the Gary guy had been nice enough to ask about. He pulled a box of ammo off the shelf, Buck knew which group he supported. One thing was sure, he didn't have to worry about bringing the dogs together for their own protection. Tonight they would do a better job strung out in the dark.

*****

The Septon soldier worked his way around the back of the place. He'd jogged slowly over the rough terrain, circling over a small knoll to get in position. In the dark it looked like the back of the cabin was windowless. He didn't even need to worry about the lack of cover. He stepped out slowly, heading for the cabin. He wasn't sure what it was that he stepped into, it felt like a small trench and he lifted his foot to feel for a spot to step out the other side.

He sensed the motion – trained men will – but it came from down low which he hadn't expected. A standing man will hit you at head, or shoulder height. He turned in time to see a blur. Then he was hit hard in the leg and he felt a pain in his calf.

The soldier wanted to yell out to warn the others, but he didn't. He didn't want to alert anything else that might be here in the dark with him. He tried to reach for his gun holster as he was driven sideways to the ground. If he had been anywhere else except Alaska, he might have had a chance.

Most dogs grab on and rip and tear, but as long they had a hold of something like a leg you had time to get a gun out and fire. But these dogs were used to dealing with grizzlies and wolves, and it was all about life and death. The dog let the leg go as soon as the man started falling and was climbing for his throat before he hit the ground. Before the soldier could react, the dog clamped down on his neck and shook hard.

The old man knew that one had just gone down. The chain snap and rattling had confirmed it. Buck smiled. The man even hadn't gotten out a sound. The dog had been quick and effective. He turned his attention towards the front of the cabin. He assumed they would send one in back and one in front. It was hilarious how they all did the same thing.

The soldier coming from the front was taking his time. He didn't know what the hell was ahead of him, but he knew he was expendable. He didn't want to be dying in this isolated piece of hell. He watched carefully in front, and checked out each obstacle before going over or around it.

He looked carefully at a slight depression in the ground. He noticed it went left and right as far as he could see in the dark. Up closer, he could see it was hardly there, just a small worn area that caused a small trench. It shouldn't be a problem to cross and he stepped forward.

The soldier heard the chain move and turned towards the sound on his right. He took a step backwards away from the sound. As the blur headed towards him, he started to backpedal as it hit his legs. His scream carried a long ways in the quiet night, echoing off the hills.

He tried to move out of range of the big dog ripping at his leg. That was when the second dog struck him in the shoulder, and he went down. He had just happened to be unlucky enough to attempt to cross the perimeter right where the two dog's chains met, giving them both an opportunity to wreak havoc.

He grabbed onto a rock for leverage and screamed uncontrollably as he held the rock tight while the two dogs ripped and tore at his legs and abdomen.

He was losing his grip, and he was bleeding out and knew it was only a matter of time. He just wanted the horror to end. As he felt his fingers let go, he heard his own screaming drowned out in the muffled snarls.

At the first scream Turov had gone as stiff as the rest of the crew. *What the hell?* That wasn't a normal scream of pain, it had been more horrified than hurt. Seconds later the true screaming had begun, climbing in pitch until it had been ground out.

Twenty-five minutes and he'd lost one, and assumed, two men. He knew this was playing for keeps, but that was two men gone way too fast. He would wait for the morning to take care of this.

Buck was comfortable that the incident should keep them back for the rest of the night. He poured himself a coffee and wondered what he should do about the situation. Something about his conversation with the Collins fellow earlier in the day was bothering him.

He thought perhaps he had sounded like he didn't care about the people who'd come up here and then been attacked on their way out. It wasn't that. He had helped some of the people, but he also made sure he kept his distance. Hell, he hadn't even asked any questions about why they were there.

Now for the first time, he was wondering if he shouldn't do more.

*****

The roar of an approaching vehicle woke the whole team. Gary, Deuce, and Victor ran for the door. Everyone else scrambled to look out the building's sole window.

Standing in the yard, Gary tried to figure where the sound was coming from. In the early dawn the mechanical roar just echoed off the surrounding hills, coming at them from every direction. Suddenly, a big truck came bouncing down over the hill. Victor had taken up a shooter's stance in the middle of the road before Gary recognized the old man driving the contraption.

"It's okay, Victor. He's okay."

Gary was floored. He couldn't understand how that truck had appeared here. The Tatra 815 was a Czechoslovakian behemoth almost never seen in North America. Gary had seen them in action in the Dakar rally, and knew they were regularly used in the old Soviet Bloc. This one was an eight-by-eight which meant four axles, eight wheels and all-wheel-drive. It looked like an elephant had humped a tank.

Tatras were indestructible and able to go through anything. The twelve-cylinder diesels and fourteen-gear trannies made sure that no obstacle was insurmountable. The big boxy truck bounced up and down as Buck brought it to a stop. He was out of the truck in one quick motion, his rifle clutched in his left hand. Gary realized he was in a hurry.

"You guys gotta go. Them followers are here."

"What happened Buck?" Gary had visions of Septon's thugs attacking Buck's cabin.

"Same thing as always, they thought my place was where you guys were, and where this thing you're looking for is." Gary could see a slight smile on the old guy's face. "They were stupid enough fuckers to try approaching the cabin in the middle of the night. The dogs took two of them."

He pictured the dogs he'd seen, that wouldn't have been pretty.

"You all pack up and take this truck cross-country back to Fairbanks." Buck grabbed an old backpack out of the Tatra, and slung it over his shoulder. "It'll take a while, but you can go anywhere, and they won't be able to follow you. Just leave it at Horton's truck stop, give the keys to Bill. I'll take care or your trucks and you can get them back at Horton's when you get the chance."

Gary was stunned. He'd planned on leaving this morning, but hadn't expected Septon to be so close behind them. *How did they keep catching up?* They didn't have a lot of options if there were soldiers were out there on the road waiting. Fuck, he was starting to really hate these guys. Buck wasn't giving him much time to think.

"Gotta go now son. They'll be here shortly. I assume they're following me."

"Victor, Deuce, let's get everything loaded into this monster. Everyone, let's go."

Scrambling to gather their things didn't take long, but boosting Vanessa up to the truck cab did. Mary reached up and pulled her old body up with firm arms until she was on the step outside the cab. Mike and Geedi joined Gary and Chantal, and the cab was full. Victor and Deuce jumped up onto the rear flatbed that was surrounded by a steel frame. Hopefully the steel sheeting attached to the outside was enough to add some security.

Buck came up to the window one last time, "Got the keys to the Hummer?"

He fished them out of his pocket and dropped them down to Buck, "What're you going to do?"

"You take off cross-country heading south. Stay parallel to the road and make your way back to Fairbanks. I'm going to hope that they follow the Hummer. I'll lose them, don't worry. They're in over their heads out here."

Gary hung his body out the massive vehicle and reached down to shake Buck's hand, "Thanks Buck, we really owe you one."

"Tell me why you're here Gary, that will do."

"It sounds crazy, but some people who get migraines actually have a message in the headaches. We figured out how to read the messages. We followed them and here we are. Now you know as much as me."

Buck seemed good with that, and smacked the flat of his hand on the door in farewell, "Et-klan-ne-te-a."

The old guy headed to the Hummer, started the truck up and spun gravel everywhere as he fishtailed out of the mine heading north.

Gary didn't waste time, sticking the Tatra in first gear and letting out the clutch. The truck lurched forward inches at a time and he realized the thing was all torque and built for strength. He changed up a few gears and the truck bounced a bit as it rocked on its suspension.

If he recalled correctly, these trucks didn't have a frame on the bottom that could break or warp. They only had a spine down the centre designed with the flexibility of a cat. This way the truck could twist to the right up front while twisting to the left in the back as it crawled over things. But it was no speed demon.

They rumbled out of the mine site and turned the truck south, staying roughly parallel to the road. As they went around behind a large knoll they lost sight of the mine. Gary was focused on keeping the truck on the best footing possible as they crawled over rock and through the muskeg at a steady pace.

From the top of the hill Turov could see the diesel smoke of the truck the old man drove off with. He hadn't seen the vehicle as it drove away earlier, but the roar of the engine he was hearing now was clearly the same. He could also see the Hummer heading north around the lake and knew he had to make a decision. Which one to follow? Where were the targets?

He ordered the second truck to race and catch up to the Hummer. They could confirm who was in that truck while Turov and his crew kept an eye on the big machine and guarded the only way out.

As the big truck moved out of sight behind a larger hill, he knew he had to move to keep up with it. He wished he could get closer and see inside. He ordered his men into the pickup and they turned around to try and follow the trail of smoke.

They drove for a bit before gaining a new vantage point. The Tatra was coming up a small valley and should pass by relatively close. He called out for someone to bring him a rifle.

*****

Gary was feeling pretty good at the wheel, getting the hang of the big Tatra, when there was a crash in the cab. Then a scream. He looked around, trying to figure out what had just happened. Vanessa was covered in blood from a hole in her chest. Shit, she'd just been shot.

Gary looked around for the hole and realized a bullet came in through the roof. The shooter was up high, which was bad. He could shoot again. The slow moving truck was a big target. He jerked the wheel and headed towards the base of the hill. This time he heard a gun go off in the back of the Tatra. Victor was trying to buy him some time.

Turov hadn't expected return fire, and ducked back as the spray of gravel exploded nearby. Well that answered one thing. There was at least one driver and one shooter in the vehicle. Some, or all, of the targets were in the big truck.

Turov lined up and fired another shot. He didn't aim as well as he should have, because he saw the flash of another round coming his way. When he looked down again he couldn't see the truck because the hill was now too steep to see the base. He could hear the thing though and it was still moving.

Inside of the truck was pandemonium as Mike freaked out, yelling for help. Vanessa had passed out and Gary knew it wasn't good. He couldn't stop, or they might all be shot. He turned to Chantal, "Do something!"

"We are," she shot back. "Just get us the fuck out of here."

Mary was trying to balance herself, holding on to Vanessa as Gary climbed the big truck over and through anything in his way. Chantal had torn off her hoodie, using it to apply pressure to the wound, trying to make the bleeding stop. Once or twice he thought he was going to get stuck, or not make it over a bank or cliff, and was amazed at the capability of the Tatra.

He figured he was still too close to the road, and made an effort to get farther away. He didn't want to see the shooter again. Once the Tatra rounded another hill a little farther from the road he was able to slow it down and try to keep the big truck level. "Okay, how are we doing back there?"

"She's gone Gary. Vanessa's gone."

No one said anything. What was there to say? It was insane. He had known in the back of his head that there was a chance of this happening. You don't screw around with companies like Septon who played for keeps and come out unscathed.

Right now he just wanted to get to Fairbanks and on to Arizona.

*****

Buck waited until he was sure the bad guys were following him. He'd had to slow down on the first few hills and wait until he saw them coming. He could tell they were in a hurry as he finally put the gas to the Hummer. He didn't want them catching up too soon. That wouldn't fit with his plan.

For the first couple hours he kept well ahead of them because he knew the road. He went hunting out this way often, and knew where the big holes and tight turns were. His followers were hell bent on catching up though and the old man pressed to keep his lead.

When Buck found the spot he was looking for, he gambled he'd be up the small track to the left and on top of the hill before they came around the corner. He kept the Hummer moving, scampering up and over the top. He stopped up there on a big plateau and waited for the pickup truck to come around the corner.

The truck came bouncing around the corner throwing dust and gravel. They didn't slow down, flying right past the small trail that Buck had taken. Now he looked out over the valley below. He knew there were caribou herding down there, and he waited until the truck slowed down when they realized the Hummer wasn't in front of them any -more.

Buck hoped the sight of the caribou spread out in front of them would be stunning enough to cause a moment's hesitancy. That's all he needed. He leaned over the Hummer's hood and brought the rifle's scope to his eye. One thing Buck could still do well was shoot. That was a skill you needed to survive out here. He shot out the front tire first and before it settled, he took out the back one as well.

Three men jumped out of the truck and hid on the far side of the vehicle. A couple of them sent bullets towards the plateau, but Buck wasn't too worried. He continued with his plan. A couple more shots into the pickup encouraged them to waste their ammo.

When a pair of them decided to try and make a move towards the hill, Buck put a couple of quick ones into the rocks at their feet and they backed up. He hoped they didn't figure out he wasn't going to kill them. He just wanted to waste some time.

Next he shot a caribou and it dropped where it stood, sixty yards from the pickup. Then he shot another. The herd was getting worked up and restless but they wouldn't run until something chased them and they knew which way to go. Right now they didn't know what was going on.

These men would have no idea what he was doing, but would try to wait him out. It was late afternoon when Buck noticed something out of the corner of his eye. *Here we go.*

He had counted on the fact that the wolf pack roaming this territory was never far from the herd. His work here was done. The ten or eleven members of the pack were healthy. These outsiders were a couple hundred miles from his place and many more from Fairbanks. Once the wolves picked up the scent of the downed caribou they wouldn't be able to ignore the easy prey. He wondered how much ammunition those boys had left. He chuckled to himself, he wasn't worried about seeing them again.

CHAPTER 30

A single phone call. That's what started this whole thing. A single phone call asking for a simple favour. Just a ride to the subway.

Ivan hadn't heard from Victor or Gary in days. He knew they were isolated, but still he wanted an update. He'd been restless for a week now.

Now he was not only dealing with Septon, but Victor was gone, and someone that he didn't know was calling him from Russia.

That was what was really bothering him, he wasn't in complete control anymore. It drove him nuts and he was itching to do something, one way or the other. What he really needed was more information on everything, because that gave him some level of control and the ability to make the right moves. Right now he couldn't do a damned thing.

When the special cell phone in his pocket went off he jumped a fraction and grabbed it quickly. Then he stalled, taking a breath before answering.

"Allo."

"Ivan, do you recognize the voice?"

He did, it was the same voice, "Da."

"I assume you have resources. Supplies, men?"

"Da." Ivan wished he knew where this conversation was going.

"Good. You will meet a flight coming in to JFK." The caller supplied a date and time.

"How will I recognise you?"

"Don't worry. I will recognise you."

He was waiting for more when he realized that the call had disconnected. Jesus, the guy was coming to New York and he wanted a team. Ivan had been at this too long to take anything at face value. He wished Victor was here now that things were heating up.

Finally he made a decision, he would transfer some money around, and make sure he had his papers in order. He wanted to ensure he had a back door escape. He was going to have to be on his toes for the next while.

*****

Alexi was becoming enraged. He was losing patience with everyone and everything. Turov hadn't called in and he had no idea what was happening. He needed to know that Collins hadn't figured the message out yet. Alexi had all his irons in the fire. He wasn't just waiting for Turov and the crews.

He pushed Gusev to take the experiments to another level. Collins had figured it out. So they should be able to.

For weeks Gusev had been inflicting migraines and then keeping the suffers agitated. The laboratory was engulfed in blinding, flashing light as the subjects were tied down to the chairs.

The young doctor made his way around the circle, stopping at each chair, screaming at each subject. Alexi watched him jab a subject with an electric rod.

But no matter how devious and sadistic Gusev was, it didn't change the subject's visions, or make them any more able to tell their tormentor what to do with them. He wouldn't admit it, but somewhere deep down Alexi was certain this was all they would ever get. It was up to someone with intelligence to put the whole puzzle together.

All the information was there. If he could just understand how that bastard Collins had figured it out in such a short time. He had been working on it for years, and now this asshole comes into the picture, nailing it in a couple weeks.

Obviously it had been a mistake to think the subjects knew what to do with the messages. The more he thought about it, the more he realized he'd had the information all along. At the very least, as much as Collins had to play with. This could have been figured out years ago if he could do whatever Collins did. It was infuriating.

Alexi watched Gusev administer the rod to one of the subjects and felt some of the stress ease. He wanted to handle the electric rod himself.

*****

The team stopped before dark and buried Vanessa. It wasn't an easy decision, or very popular with Mike. He had been rebuffing her advances for the whole trip, but she had been wearing him down. Now he was distraught, angry with himself for giving her a hard time.

They had all understood that it made no sense to involve the authorities at this point. It would only slow them down, and with Septon around, they needed to keep moving fast.

In the morning the mood had been quiet and reflective. No one spoke much as they cleaned out the interior of the truck and reloaded their gear.

Gary had been slow crawling through sand, mud, and rock most of the day. The Tatra rose up in the air as they went up over a ledge, or crawled up out of a hole, the front wheels dangling. The other wheels kept turning as the Tatra balanced on the edge, finally falling forward onto its front wheels while the back ones dangled behind over open space.

He was sure they were almost in Fairbanks and angled for the main road which was a mile or so off to the right. As he came down over a knoll and onto the highway he watched carefully for any movement in the distance. The coast seemed clear as they pulled onto the asphalt.

He hadn't gone much more than twenty or thirty miles an hour the last five hours, and now he was able to open up the Tatra. The big machine was rumbling along at about fifty-five when Septon struck.

*****

Turov had been wondering all morning about Petrov and his crew that had followed the Hummer north on the dirt road. They hadn't come back or reported in. He had to let that go and concentrate on the big truck.

They had kept track up until dark by stopping regularly and listening for the diesel engine in the distance. They had been sure it had stopped for the night when it went quiet. He had kept his men on shifts all night to make sure the targets didn't start up and leave in the middle of the night. When the machine had begun moving this morning, they had continued to track it.

Turov had been sitting on a hill, watching as the big truck came out from behind some hills and worked its way up to the road. It kicked up big cloud of dust as it took off down the road into Fairbanks. It was time, he yelled to the men to get loaded up.

Including himself, the team was now down to four guys and since one was driving, that left him with just two soldiers. He ordered one of them to shoot out the tires of the machine when they got close enough.

*****

Gary felt the difference in the handling immediately. First one side, then the other, he knew something had happened. He tried to see behind the vehicle, but the Tatra was so damned big that the mirrors showed very little. Then he caught sight of Deuce waving at him in the side mirror. He was pointing to the road behind them and making the shape of a gun with his hand.

Septon. *Shit*, he had to think fast. They must have shot out the back tires. Thankfully it wouldn't slow them down. The Tatra would lose some traction, but with six out of eight tires still working, it was good to go on the pavement. But running didn't seem like the way to go. They couldn't outrun Septon on the road.

Gary started to gear down. He brought the truck down to a crawl and then stopped on the shoulder. The dust swirled around the truck, and while everyone was waiting for it to settle Mike crawled over Chantal and dropped out of the left side of the Tatra.

"Mike, get back here. Mike!"

Gary couldn't believe that he'd jumped out, but then he should have guessed. After Vanessa's shooting, Mike might do anything. In the mirror he saw Mike reach down and pick up a large rock and head back behind the truck.

"Victor. Cover him," he yelled out the window.

Turov was watching the back of the truck stopped on the side of the road when he saw someone walking towards them. He wasn't sure what to think. When he realized the guy was carrying something in his hand he yelled, "Shoot him, shoot him!"

Turov watched as the man raised his hand and hurled something at their truck. At the same time the man spun backwards, thrown to the ground as a bullet slammed through his chest. Suddenly there was a loud thud and their windshield shattered. Then Turov felt the bullets hitting their pickup. They needed to get out of the vehicle and secure the targets.

*****

Gary heard the shots from in the back of the Tatra and knew Victor and Deuce were taking care of business. Worried about Mike he put the Tatra in reverse.

"Get down as low as you can and stay there." he yelled to everyone in the cab.

He revved the engine and big columns of smoke poured from the exhaust stacks. Then Gary nailed the pedal and sent the big truck jerking backwards.

Gary didn't see the Septon crew trying to get out of their truck, or the driver's face once he'd realized the big machine was coming at them. Unsure if he should move the truck out of the way, the driver jumped from the vehicle as the Tatra struck it in the front corner.

Gary felt the impact and slowed the vehicle. Using their momentum and a little fuel he kept the Tatra going backwards. He felt it lift off the ground, tilting up on the one side. He knew he'd had to have done significant damage to the pickup truck's front end. *Good enough.* He could have backed right over it, but they didn't have time to waste. So with everyone hugging the floor in the big beast he shifted into forward and rolled off the damaged pickup. Hopefully it was out of commission.

Deuce reloaded the gun Victor had given him, and the two of them kept shooting the whole time that Gary was backing up and then pulling forward. Septon's guys were firing back, but the steel sides of the Tatra shielded them during the running battle. Finally, the massive truck engine screamed as Gary started to pull away from the battle zone.

Gary felt badly about not stopping, but it was clear that Mike was gone, they couldn't do anything for him now, and time was everything. He could tell Chantal was crying silently beside him and he couldn't do anything about that either. He up-shifted and kept the pedal down.

*****

Turov had been firing from his position on the ground at the side of the road. He wasn't getting killed on this mission. He wasn't stupid.

He was getting closer to completing it though. He knew they had to hurry up and get back to town. That would take at least an hour or more at a steady run.

The targets were now down two people. That should hamper their efforts. He had replacements, but they didn't. He just had to make sure they didn't make it to the end before he caught them.

*****

Gary hadn't realized they were so close to town and was relieved when they pulled into Fairbanks. People on the roadside looked at the Tatra like it was a monster when he asked for directions to Horton's garage.

"Bill?"

"Yes, who are you?" He seemed confused by these people climbing out of Buck's truck.

"Gary Collins. Buck said to drop the truck and keys with you."

Bill blinked. He figured if this bunch weren't on Buck's good side it was stupid to show up here. He nodded.

"Buck said you could probably point us to someone that flies Charters around here." Gary asked as he handed over the keys.

He was lying, but he would have asked Buck about it if he'd thought of it back then. Since he was thinking of it now, he was sure Buck wouldn't mind him using his name.

Bill took his time to answer, "Come on in the office, I got a few numbers there."

*****

Turov and his men stood in the living room of the house of the air traffic controller who had worked the day shift. He'd wanted simple information. Just when and where they had gone.

He hadn't been happy after jogging for almost two hours to discover the Tatra parked in plain sight at a gas station and the targets long gone. His contact told him that the targets had headed to an airfield and left in a small plane. Dammit, *shit,* where had they gone?

That question brought them to this man's house at the supper hour to have a frank conversation. The man had been quick to offer up the information he was looking for. Now Turov had to decide how to leave things.

Killing the guy was an option, but that would draw unnecessary attention and would mean he'd have to kill a few more, including the guy at the gas station who'd sold them the rifles and the guy who'd done the tracking for them. Too many loose ends to clean up quickly. Shit, he didn't even know where Petrov's crew was yet.

He didn't have time for this shit. He decided to offer the guy money as an incentive to keep quiet.

"Look, you've had a bad day and now you're gonna get a chance to put some money in your pocket in exchange for your silence. But you have to ask yourself '*who are these people walking around with wads of cash who have the nerve to kidnap an air traffic controller.*'" Turov thought about it for a moment. "You'd also have to ask yourself if there was any safe place to hide if you thought it wasn't best to just take the money and let the world go back to normal."

He wasn't really surprised when the man took the money. Now he was obligated to keep quiet. Turov hoped for his sake that he did. Now that he knew the targets were flying to Anchorage, a short hop from Fairbanks, he wondered what was happening there.

CHAPTER 31

Gary and Chantal had both been on their phones looking for flights out of Anchorage. After they landed, the pilot of the small charter they had hired to get them that far asked around and found them a flight. The gambling junket to Las Vegas didn't mind the team taking up some of their empty seats. The rest of the plane was filled with military guys and gold miners taking a weekend off to party and gamble.

With time to kill before the flight, Gary had taken a walk. He ended up down by the harbor sitting on a bench thinking things through. He was startled when a voice broke the quiet. "Hello there! Is this Anchorage?"

Gary had looked around, it sounded like the voice had carried across the water. Straining his eyes he picked out an object floating just offshore. The odd shaped thing was too low and long for a small boat. Gary couldn't figure out what the hell he was looking at. Was it a threat?

"Yes, this is Anchorage, Alaska." He coughed, almost embarrassed to ask, "What are you floating on?"

The older man laughed, "It's a submarine."

As his eyes adjusted to the dimming light, he could pick out the silhouette of someone sitting in a lawn chair on top of a sub just drifting slowly by. The thing wasn't big enough to be military and had to be a personal sub. Something still didn't seem right as he realized it was drifting away.

"That's one strange looking submarine," he yelled.

The man laughed as he drifted out of sight, "It's made out of concrete."

Gary wasn't sure if that had just happened, but a concrete submarine was just ridiculous. He shook his head, God he was tired. He headed back to the airport with the picture of the concrete submarine drifting away stuck in his mind.

Gary and Chantal curled up and tried to sleep a bit on the flight. He couldn't speak for anyone else but he was exhausted. Hopefully they'd given Septon the slip.

Victor rented a vehicle so they could keep Gary and Chantal's names off the paperwork, and they drove out of Las Vegas into the desert towards Arizona. Once they had some distance between them and Las Vegas, Gary just wanted to be out of the state and into Arizona before he stopped. Once they crossed into Arizona at Lake Mead, he started looking for a small hotel.

He didn't want to use one, but everyone had spent the previous couple nights cramped in the Tatra or trying to catch a couple hours on the plane. With no one following them, they should be able to relax for the rest of the night. They all needed rest for whatever was coming next.

It was nearly two a.m. when they pulled into Kingman. Gary let Chantal settle in and went looking for Deuce and Victor. "Deuce can you bring the trigger stuff to your room? I'll get Geedi."

Pinned to the wall was the map of Arizona they grabbed at the rental agency. Gary hadn't bothered to bring the women to this session. This was about fine-tuning the location, and they'd already confirmed the women wouldn't help there. It was about the bars that Mike and Geedi saw at this stage, and now it was just Geedi.

This was the first time they were going after the visions without Mike, and Gary hoped everything still worked the way it was supposed to.

The flashing lights and noise was getting to Geedi as he kept his head down and let it aggravate him to the point he felt the throbbing begin. Finally he gave Gary a signal that things had begun and moved to a spot that seemed the right distance from the map on the wall.

"I see the bar Gary. It is still in northern Arizona, same as when we were in Alaska."

"Is there anything around the area it's pointing to?"

Geedi squinted and moved forward slightly, "North of those mountains there." Gary got closer to the map and had the boy direct his finger to the spot. "There, that's it."

Shit, this was as isolated as Alaska had been. The spot was right on Arizona's border with Utah in the mountains and canyons near Vermillion Cliffs, which was almost part of the Grand Canyon. *Christ, what's next?*

*****

Turov was at least a couple hours behind the targets, which wasn't bad under the circumstances. But he was pissed. The targets weren't supposed to get out of Alaska. Now he had to find them again.

The plane that Septon had flown in on was fuelled and ready to go. They had stopped in Anchorage and discovered that the targets had boarded a gambling charter headed for Vegas. Setting down in Las Vegas about two hours after the targets, his men headed right to the rental agencies.

One thing Turov had lots of was money to spread around. Alexi never ran out of it. Luckily rentals at this time of night were slow and it was easy to discover that a Russian had rented a white passenger van. The big bonus was when the agent mentioned that the guy had also picked up a map of Arizona.

The Septon crew rented a pair of SUVs, and now Turov was just across the border into Arizona trying to decide what to do. He couldn't let the targets get any further away, and yet he didn't want to race right past them if they were stopped someplace for the night. He told the crew to keep watching for the van as they took their time cruising slowly past hotels and rest stops.

Turov knew he had to update the boss. He had been avoiding the phone call for days now. He pictured Alexi sitting there fuming, waiting for the call. He took a deep breath and pulled out his cell.

"What is it?"

He could hear the anger in Alexi's voice, "It's Turov. I'm finally able call you."

"What the fuck is going on Turov?" Alexi shouted into the phone.

"They went to an old abandoned mine north of Fairbanks. They slipped past us and we've followed them to Arizona." Turov stalled briefly and then lied, "we are trailing them now."

"And there are no fucking telephones in Alaska?" Alexi sounded pissed. "Why haven't you stopped them yet?"

"Everything is going as planned boss. I've eliminated two of their team and will continue to reduce it until there are none left."

"Why only two Turov? Why didn't you stop them all at once."

Turov had to be careful with this one. The appearance of incompetence could be costly. "This leader of theirs has the advantage of knowing where he is going and we don't. But we'll get them."

"Just get them soon. But understand that you must deliver on this. Got that?"

"Yes sir, I'll deliver."

"Good. Keep me posted regularly now that you're back where they have phones."

Turov rode in silence after the call, watching scenery roll past as dawn broke across the desert. They weren't making much progress down the road as the driver kept stopping and checking little side roads and other spots the targets might have pulled over to stop for the night.

"There it is," one of his soldiers yelled.

Sure enough, they rolled by a small motel and there was the white van. It might not be the right one, but he was betting money it was. He instructed the driver to find the next side road and park back from the corner. He wanted well off the main road so the white van wouldn't see them when they headed out. One of his men could watch for the targets from the shrubs lining the road.

He had a feeling this thing was finally going to end. He could almost see the big bonus the boss would give him.

*****

Ivan was at the airport picking up his mystery caller from Russia. He'd gone over the scenario again and again and decided to let it play out. He had really wanted to ask his bosses about the caller, but knew that in the long run his loyalty would be questioned for not just keeping his mouth shut and obeying.

This could be a hit in the making, but it could also be opportunity knocking. If this man was in with his bosses, or even higher above them, then this was an opportunity to show his abilities here and maybe get other chances in the future.

But if this man was not in with his bosses, the man's access to his special phone number meant his bosses had found trouble, which also could affect his business. Briefly he thought of running. Putting some stuff together and disappearing. He knew he could do it, but it wasn't the lifestyle for him. He liked being the leader, liked walking around with everyone knowing he was in charge. He'd liked that feeling since the first time he felt it as a teenager. He didn't plan on letting go now.

Now he was working a different plan, he had some of his men strategically placed around the airport, ready to roll. He would control as many of the variables as he could.

Finally, he put himself out in the open in the arrivals section of the airport and waited for the passengers from the flight from Russia to clear customs and pick up their luggage.

Carefully he eyed every passenger that came through the door. He was sure he would recognise his target before the man walked up to him. When it seemed that everyone had picked up their luggage and exited, someone stepped up beside him.

"Ivan, glad you were able to pick me up."

He turned quickly, an old man stood beside him watching the other travellers walk past. Ivan wondered where he came from, and was sure it wasn't off this flight from Russia. The weather-beaten face had the scars of history written all over it. There was no doubt that this was his caller. "I'm glad you recognised me."

"No. You're not happy that I know who you are. I can appreciate that feeling. But don't worry, you'll know everything in good time." The old man laughed and stuck his hand out, "Igor."

Ivan shook the offered hand, astonished to notice that the old man's third finger was missing. The same one as Alexi. That could be a problem. He couldn't help but think the two men had history together.

"Alright Ivan, gather your men and take me somewhere where we can talk in private."

That Igor had spotted his men shocked him. There wasn't much choice at this point as he led his new guest out to the waiting car.

CHAPTER 32

Gary had everyone up and on the road first thing in the morning. Their only stop had been for gas and a map of the Grand Canyon. Gary was sure they would need it. He still didn't have a clue how they were supposed to find something in the canyon.

They passed the towns of Cameron and Tuba, entering the Navajo Indian reservation.

The canyon itself was part of the Colorado River system, running southwest from Powell Lake to Lake Mead. For a couple hundred miles the canyon and its cliffs on either side were so long and steep that it could take days to climb down and you could only get back out in certain places.

There was a National Monument at Vermillion Cliffs near the top of the canyon, so Gary knew that there had to be parking.

There weren't a lot of vehicles around when the rental van pulled to the empty end of the parking lot. They parked as far as they could get from the tourist stands selling local native crafts and where the tribe gathered a fee for entry onto the trails that led along the top of the cliffs.

Mary and Chantal were quick to jump out and spark up their smokes. Geedi headed towards one of the craft tables while

Deuce and Victor stretched their legs and looked around. Gary went over to talk to the guy taking the entrance fees. The old Navajo had a face tanned to leather, and wore his long gray hair loose, hanging around his shoulders.

"Hello. Great day we have today," Gary was unsure how to break the ice.

"Yah'eh-the, the sun is happy today." The old man hardly looked at Gary, "You are here to see the cliffs?"

"I'm actually not sure. We kind of ended up here at the end of a long journey, but maybe we do need to see the cliffs."

This seemed to wake up the old Navajo, his eyes opened wider as he looked over Gary's shoulder at the rest of the team wandering around the parking lot. His next question seemed to be formed slowly and deliberately, "You came here with these people, and you don't know why?"

"I know that sounds a little strange, but we're on a trip, just stopping in different places along the way."

"Where did you come from?"

"Fairbanks, Alaska," Gary didn't see any point in lying.

"You have travelled from the land of the Dené to the land of the Diné."

Gary blinked. He wasn't getting the point to this conversation.

"Yah'eh-teh," the old man repeated.

Ah … Gary attempted to pronounce the word Buck had said when they shook hands goodbye. "Et-klan-ne-te-a."

The old Indian stared at Gary for a moment and nodded, "You and your group should be taking the western trail along the cliffs. It starts over there." He pointed to a sliver of an opening between two rock walls at the end of the parking lot.

As he headed back to the van the others noticed and met him there. They had become accustomed to Gary letting them know what was coming next.

"It looks like we go for a walk now. Victor, get the supplies ready. Everyone else sort your personal stuff and decide what you can carry easily." God, he hoped this would be over soon. They were starting to look like a pretty worn-out bunch.

When a new truck came sliding into the parking lot they all turned to watch, nerves still on edge. Before they could react, the truck veered towards them, the driver swung the truck sideways as he braked and skidded to a stop. Two men with guns jumped out.

One of them took charge and yelled the stupidest thing Gary'd heard in a while. "Freeze, no one move!"

This one wasn't in charge because he kept looking back at the truck, so Gary knew the boss was still inside. Deuce jumped in front of the two women and tried to push them towards the far side of their white rental van.

The guys with the guns seemed comfortable that they were in charge of the situation and one-stepped towards Chantal, while the other stayed back and covered his buddy.

When Geedi, who was the only one not to have re-joined the team at the van, walked up and asked, "What's going on here?" Everything went to hell.

The man moving on Chantal looked at Geedi as if he wasn't sure the kid was one of the targets or not. He sure didn't look harmful. The guy addressed his back up, "Grab that kid, hold him."

The second soldier looked at Geedi and then back at the big black man guarding woman. He knew who he had to keep an eye on. He took a few quick steps and reached out to grab the kid.

Gary watched it unfold like it had been choreographed. Geedi sidestepped the thug's hand and used a perfect grab-and-jerk on the guy's arm to send him reeling forward, off balance. Gary was moving before he realized it himself. He stepped forward and struck out.

Victor used the confusion to make his move from behind the van. He went for the threat closest to Chantal. Shooting the guy in the head at close range, he kept walking right over top of his victim, while firing rounds at Septon's SUV.

"Back up! Back up!" Someone in the SUV shouted at the driver. As the SUV tore out of the parking lot, Victor kept shooting until he had no bullets left.

Gary kicked his opponent's feet out from under him and came down hard with a pair of blows to the guy's head. He wanted him out cold, but couldn't bring himself to kill him.

Chantal and Mary were trying to clean off some of the blood that had splattered on them when Victor had shot Septon's guy. Gary knew that Septon was trying to end it here. They had come in hard and ready to have it out, they didn't seem concerned about operating in public this time.

"Let's get out of here." The team needed to move fast.

They grabbed their bags and headed for the hole in the cliff at the end of the parking lot. The undisturbed dirt said this was an unused trail. He wanted to get out of sight before Septon came back and saw where they went.

What they hadn't seen was the old Navajo watching the whole thing. The old man summoned a kid from one of the other

264   REJEAN GIGUERE

booths and gave him instructions. The youngster raced off though another hole in the cliff wall.

The old man knew what was coming next. Sure enough, three men carrying guns walked into the parking lot without a vehicle. They came straight to his booth and started asking questions.

"Where did that group of people go?

"What group?"

Their leader raised his gun and shot the old native in the chest twice. Turning to the next booth he asked. "Where did the other group go?"

The old Navajo lay on the sand at the bottom of his booth. His life wasn't ending as he'd envisioned. Like others before him, he'd been destined to guard the gate. As he listened to the women screaming at the next booth he realized that he hadn't succeeded. He was talking to his ancestors as he took his last breath.

*****

Septon's guard came out to talk to the five-ton's driver as the truck stopped at the front gate. He was caught by surprise when someone quietly dropped out the back of the truck and ran to his side with a gun.

They backed the guard into the security hut and opened the gates. Everything looked good so far. Ivan hoped anyone monitoring the cameras missed the action and it just looked like the guard opened the gate.

The five-ton drove around to the garage area near the loading dock. The man in the passenger seat jumped out and pounded on the delivery door. Once he was buzzed in, he held the door open.

The five-ton's rear door rolled up quickly and a dozen more men jumped out, hustling through the door. Ivan and Igor climbed out last and followed their men. Inside the facility security was at a minimum. This place was designed to keep people out, but once they were inside Septon seemed to rely on cameras and a few security staff, that was about it.

Ivan knew the biggest risk was not knowing how many of Septon's soldiers were still in the garage area. That's why his men targeted it first. He heard shots, and arrived to find three men dead on the floor.

"Okay, they'll know we're here. You know your assignments. Go!"

Ivan and Igor hung back and let the men do their work. One team headed to secure the offices in the front of the building, with instructions to find the old man. All his men had photos, so he was sure they knew who Alexi was.

The second crew split up, searching out the security stations and making sure all the staff were accounted for. Ivan and Igor heard some shots and an alarm start ringing. After a short fire-fight the alarm went out and it was quiet again.

A third crew was looking for the prisoners and any doctors that were working for Septon. The experiments had to stop immediately. Ivan would wait to hear word from his men before he and Igor walked any further into the large building.

Igor didn't say much, but when he did speak, there was a chilling authority there. It was like how some people looked as bad as they were. Like the ones you saw on television being marched into court and you knew the second you saw them they were bad.

That was what it felt like to Ivan. It seeped out of the old man somehow. Finally he got a call from his men searching through the offices. They hadn't found anything. Ivan ordered them to join up with the others checking security.

That turned out to be unnecessary when he got a wrap up call from that crew saying they had the place nailed down and were on the security cameras. Ivan had only one question then, "Where is the owner Alexi?"

"Team three just found him and a doctor."

*****

Alexi and Gusev had heard the internal alarms start and then shut off. Although Alexi had been briefly concerned, he had returned to helping Gusev get better results from the subjects. The thick soundproofed walls prevented them from hearing the bullets being fired.

They had been working with Sergi because he was so new to the program, fresh was the best description. Sergi might have been right that his headaches had been just starting, but Gusev was sure he could make them more regular and knew that Sergi was tough enough to take it.

When the men had burst through the door Alexi had been shocked, then his anger kicked in. Who in the hell were these guys? And where the fuck was his security? The sound of one of the intruders speaking in Russian made a click go off in his head, and he was instantly alarmed.

It appeared that these men were just securing the area, waiting for their boss. When Alexi went to stand up he was slapped hard across the face. At his age that was enough to twist him around, nearly knocking him to the ground.

*****

Ivan had wanted to get his hands on Alexi for a while now. But before he shut the guy down, he wanted to find out who he was and where he got his money. Now he was equally interested in knowing why Igor was so eager for a piece of Alexi. Something told Ivan he would want to watch this.

He stepped into the room first, momentarily blocking their captive's view. As Ivan stood aside, Alexi's angry look changed.

Alexi's face froze, then he involuntarily coughed, or perhaps it was a choke. It was hard to tell. Looking from one old man to the other, Ivan quickly realized the two men were about the same age. They looked identical except for Alexi's messy grey hair. As the color drained out of Alexi's face, it too turned grey.

"It has been a long time Alexi Tambov. Or perhaps I should say Alexi Tanovich."

Interesting. These two must know each other well.

"You should have known that keeping Alexi as your first name was a mistake. Either way, it was only a matter of time. Now we have some catching up to do don't we?"

Ivan could see the panic appear on Alexi's face.

While Igor instructed the team to strap Alexi down in the chair and tie his hands flat to the surface of the table, Alexi squirmed and struggled. Finally, the old man turned and ordered everyone out of the room. "You stay Ivan."

Once everyone was out Igor again spoke, "Ivan, today you watch and learn a lesson. A lesson about loyalty and honour. Watch how the code works and how the code lasts forever."

Ivan stood back, leaning against the door.

"So my old friend, we finally catch up to you." Igor pulled a chair up to the table and took a seat. "You angered a lot of people when you took off with all of our secrets. We were all supposed to benefit equally from the spoils of war and the riches of criminals."

Alexi tried reasoning with his captor, "I needed to get out like everyone else, it wasn't safe."

"You didn't need to take all our files that included the bank accounts with all the money we were sitting on." Igor seemed to be getting worked up.

"Igor, honestly, it wasn't like that."

"It's okay Alexi, we fix it today." He opened up a small leather pouch and took out some documents. He placed them on the table, then he pulled out some metal tools from the same case and placed them beside the papers.

Ivan was getting more and more interested. He was certain that the place to be was watching, not participating. Alexi on the other hand didn't appear to want to watch or participate, as beads of sweat formed on his forehead.

"I have some paperwork for you to sign my friend, and I assume you will be cooperative." Igor reached forward and moved one of the tools closer.

Alexi merely nodded.

"You were always the sadist among us. We did it for our country, or sometimes for the money, but you enjoyed it. Even I was ashamed by the ends you went to." Igor smiled, "But I see you recognise your favourite tool from the old days." Igor pushed the implement another inch towards Alexi.

The tool looked like a scalpel with a circular blade. Ivan watched Alexi staring at it. Igor asked him to release Alexi's right hand. The old man turned the paperwork around and told Alexi to sign all the marked spots.

Powers of attorney, ownerships for all his assets and accounts. Stacks of legal documents. He was losing everything, and Alexi couldn't figure out how they had gotten all the information. Slowly, with a shaking hand he picked up the pen and signed his name in all the required places.

Igor asked Ivan to tie Alexi's arm back to the table. He leaned forward, his elbows taking his weight, looking into his old friend's eyes. "Do you remember the oath we all took when we each cut off our own finger?"

He held his hand up and showed his own missing finger, "There were only nine of us, so we each cut off a finger as a symbol." He nodded his head as if remembering, "We all agreed that anyone who betrayed the group would lose their remaining fingers before they died."

He reached for the circular tool. "I don't care about getting my finger Alexi, but there are eight men back in Russia who absolutely want theirs. I said I would oblige them."

Alexi struggled against the ropes as Igor reached forward and grabbed his left hand, separating one of the fingers. He placed the tool in around the base of the finger and looked into Alexi's face. Holding the hand in place, he twisted and curled his wrist, then with a jerk and a tug the bloody finger plopped onto the table.

"That's one. Seven more."

Ivan watched as Alexi almost fainted, swaying in pain and hysteria. Igor robotically sliced off seven more fingers that landed on the table. He calmly wrapped them up in cloth and placed them into his case.

Igor turned, "Wait outside please Ivan. Some pleasures we enjoy on our own. You understand?"

"I understand." Ivan looked back as he left the room and saw Igor pull a large shiny knife out of his case. The old man reached down and cut the ropes holding Alexi. Ivan noticed the restraint rings five feet off the floor, and as he pulled the door closed he watched Igor drag Alexi by the hair towards the wall.

CHAPTER 33

Gary and the team squeezed through the rocky opening, coming out on a ledge that ran along the side of the canyon. He had no idea where he was going, but kept walking, trying to put some distance between their group and Septon's crew that were sure to come back.

With Gary in front and Victor in the rear, the team stretched out single file. After walking for ten minutes he still hadn't seen anything that stood out, or gave him a hint what they were supposed to do next.

The rifle shot echoed down the canyon, and Victor grunted as he went down to one knee. Gary scanned the canyon rim, but couldn't spot the shooter. Time for a management decision, "Deuce grab Victor, everyone else get going. Move. Move!"

He hoped the corner ahead of them would offer a little protection. As soon as they were past the corner he went back to look at Victor. Chantal was inspecting his wound, but it was obvious that he was going fast. The long-range rifle had done its job. He'd been hit from behind and the front of his chest was blown open.

Gary went down low and put his face close to Victor's. This man had gone down on orders from his boss for people he didn't know. He was sure the mission didn't mean much to Victor, but his honour meant everything and he was dying for it.

"You make Ivan proud, and I thank you deeply." Gary held him tight. Victor tried to speak but coughing was all he managed.

Finally he whispered, "Victor is such a better name than Boris."

He saw Victor's smile and knew he'd been heard. The life drained out of Victor and Gary slumped over his lifeless body, it hurt to see him go. He was tired. This was a good man.

Chantal had her hand on his shoulder, "We need to go."

She was right, he stood up with Victor's pistol in his hand, "They can't be far behind, let's get out of here."

The next shot rang out from within the canyon and Gary took a bullet through the arm. He was spun around, overbalancing and almost toppled off the cliff. "Go Chantal, go, go." Jesus, they were trying to kill her. Together, they ran for the next corner.

Luckily, there were more corners along the path and they were making good progress when they rounded another corner and ran into a Navajo. He pointed up, and Gary noticed the faint trail up the side of the valley.

At the top was another native motioning them to climb. Gary stepped aside and sent Mary up first. She struggled up on her hands and feet, but with Chantal's help the two women worked their way up the cliff to the trail above.

He sent Geedi up after them while Deuce quickly wrapped a strip of his torn shirt over the bullet hole in his arm. As they climbed he couldn't see anyone following. Yet. He was surprised when the Navajo followed behind him and motioned for them all to stay put.

They waited and watched until they saw three men approaching along the trail. Septon's men moved cautiously, carrying rifles in their hands. Just as he began to wonder what was going on, one of the natives whistled.

A few seconds later they could hear a roaring crash. Looking up, rocks were sliding down the side of the cliff, breaking other rocks loose, building momentum as they fell. They watched in fascinated horror as the men on the trail looked up to see the falling rocks.

Septon's men hesitated, as if they were deciding if they should go forward or back. Gary knew it was too late for that.

Turov looked up at the rocks rolling down the hillside and realized he had nowhere to go. He was a couple yards behind his two soldiers and scrambled backwards as the rocks began to hit. The other crewmembers weren't to be as lucky. They had to choose to run forward or back. They didn't know what was ahead so they turned and tried to run back along the narrow trail towards Turov as the first rocks started hitting them.

One stopped, trying to avoid a big rock sliding his way and the other soldier ran into him from behind, pushing him right into the boulder's path. The soldier swore as he tried to deflect it but the rock crashed into him hard and he was knocked backwards.

Clawing at thin air, the last thing he saw before falling off the edge was the other soldier looking at him in shock. The last soldier should have been running instead of standing still watching his buddy fall, as he was hit by one, then two, and a pile of boulders. The soldier cried out as he tumbled off the ledge bouncing off the canyon wall, down towards the Colorado River.

The two natives pointed along the upper trail. Obviously the team had to go it alone. They walked along the smaller ledge, carefully looking ahead.

The sound of another gunshot from below made them duck as they tried to see what was happening. The Navajo had appeared unarmed, so it probably meant that there was still one of Septon's men in the hunt.

Gary found a vantage point and struggled to look down into the canyon. He could just make out someone climbing up the wall to the second trail. Someone was catching up to them.

"Go, go, go." Gary pushed Chantal and Mary ahead of him.

The team was at a dead run when they suddenly came across another old grey-haired native crouched by a narrow crack in the wall. Mary, in front, stopped.

The old man moved his head in their direction, but his cloudy eyes seemed blind, "Why have you come here?"

"We are following the message." Gary had decided to play this old man straight.

"You must understand that there is no return. Once you enter you cannot come back."

Gary realized this was a warning and maybe the last chance to get off this rollercoaster ride. There was no doubt he and Chantal were going to see it through, he needed to get her to safety, but the others should have a choice.

"Look guys, I think this is the end. You each have to decide for yourselves if you're going through with whatever this is." He waved his arms to encompass the canyon, the native and the crack in the wall.

Mary opened her mouth to speak, "I'm going…"

A bullet slammed off the rock and dust scattered in the air.

"Mary, Chantal. Go," he grabbed their arms and pushed them towards the crack, they needed to get through the wall and safe.

The Indian raised his hand to momentarily stop them, "You must walk through the waterfall to find your destination."

It sounded about as bizarre as it could get, but Chantal had a hold of Mary's hand as they squeezed through the crack in the wall.

Another shot rang out and the two men and teenager all ducked instinctively. The old Indian never moved a muscle, "It is time, you must go now."

Gary pushed Deuce and Geedi ahead, "lets get the hell out of here."

"You cannot take this journey," The old man spoke again. They turned to see who he meant and were shocked to see he was pointing at Gary.

"What do you mean? Who can't go?" Gary was quick to ask.

"You. No one who is injured can take the journey." Then He pointed towards Geedi, "Nor can they go if they are less old than sixteen years."

Gary touched his injured arm, it still hurt like hell, but the bleeding had pretty well stopped. He wondered how the blind man had figured out he was injured. And how did old man know what age Geedi was.

The realization that he couldn't go on was brutal.

He could imagine the horror in Chantal's eyes once she realized he hadn't followed. He wanted to see her before she left, but everything was out of control. He had to act quickly.

"You gotta go Deuce." He grabbed the big guy in a quick hug.

"See you soon buddy. You did good Gary."

"Tell Chantal I'll be there soon. I know how it works, and as soon as I can I'll come and find her." He pushed Deuce through the crack and turned to face the shooter.

Before he could act the old man made a strange hooting signal. The sound of falling rocks started again.

"You will have no problems as you return along the ledges." The old man said as the dust settled.

*****

That was the coolest colored waterfall Deuce had ever seen. He could see Mary and Chantal's footprints leading right up to the shimmering sheet of water. He looked back once, but it was now or never. Slowly he raised his hands out in front of him.

He felt the water cascade across his hands and then up his arms. The colors in the water seemed to make it glow. He didn't think it was the coldness that was sending a tingling feeling up his arms. He really wished his sister was here with him as he pushed his head through.

*****

Slowly Gary and Geedi worked their way back to New York. He bought tickets on Amtrak that allowed them time to rest and think. He'd called Ivan and let him know that they had made it the end, and explain that Victor was gone. His friend surprised him with news that Septon was out of business. He thought about the others on the way back and hoped they hadn't died for nothing.

He kept coming back to Chantal. He'd done a lot of hard things in his time, but this had been the toughest. There was something about that cocky, stubborn woman and he was missing her already. He hadn't been lying when he'd said he was going to find her. That was going to be all that mattered once he took care of some things.

He had to just trust that Deuce could keep her safe.

*****

Geedi knew he would have to wait a bit to be able to go on the next journey, and he and Gary had agreed they would stay in touch in New York. Geedi was fascinated by all the things Gary knew and wanted to learn more from him.

They had been back a week when Gary picked him up.

"Nice car," he ran his hand over the leather seat. "Where are we going?"

"That would ruin the surprise." Gary laughed.

"Even a hint?" They were driving through a part of Brooklyn he didn't recognise.

"You'll find out when we get there." Gary just grinned.

"Will there be food?"

"God, is that all you think about?"

"No," Geedi said in a lower tone, "I think about a lot of things. I think about Septon a lot. And the headaches. I wonder about Mary and Chantal and Deuce."

Gary nodded in agreement.

"And I think about school, and what I am supposed to do with my life." He grinned, "and I think about girls. And food!"

Gary laughed as he was intended to.

By this time Geedi had no idea where they were. Finally, the car pulled up in front of a dojo.

"A dojo?" he exclaimed. "Are you going to practice with me?"

Gary shook his head, "The man I'm taking you to meet is a very good friend. You will always show him respect."

"Yes Gary, I will." Geedi suddenly became serious.

Inside they saw a bunch of kids training, while an instructor moved among them, showing a move, or correcting a technique. As they watched the group working out, they noticed one young student flipping his partner over and over. The other kid didn't seem to have a chance.

A guy who looked old like Gary came over to shake their hands. "Ivan, this is Geedi, I was hoping he could join the class."

"Hello, welcome," Ivan reached out.

Geedi couldn't believe the size of him, but his gaze focused on the tattoos. He felt his hand swallowed up by the stocky man's grip.

"Let's see what you can do. How about wrestling with one of my students?"

"Okay, no problem." Geedi's blood started to pump, he was going to get to show how much he had been practicing.

Ivan called out the kid who had been flipping his partner. The two of them squared off and started trying to pin each other to the mat. The young Russian was quick to attack but Geedi was equally quick to counter. After the first couple feints the two started to get more serious. Those watching could hear the blows being snuck in as the boys continued to wrestle.

Gary was caught somewhere between the past and the future, he was going somewhere soon but he had no idea where. Ivan had a brand new facility to add to his holdings and was on top of the world.

"Does this remind you of anything Gary?" Ivan asked. "It brings back memories."

Gary smiled, watching the two young boys fighting it out.

"Yes, it sure does."

EPILOGUE

Chantal wasn't sure if she lost consciousness, but she definitely had experienced something truly bizarre. Like she was thinning out and expanding. It was like she could feel her own cells and tissues at a molecular level. She wasn't sure if she was even whole anymore. She lost track of time and space, until suddenly she was floating through darkness towards another waterfall. Finally, she felt her feet beneath her as she became whole again. Then her hands were in front of her, breaking through the water. Now hesitating, thinking of Gary, she stepped through.

The bright lights of the big room were disorientating. When she saw Mary she relaxed slightly. Blinking, she tried to focus on the voice. "Well, it looks like you passed the test. Welcome to Earth Two."

The man in the white uniform sat at a perfectly white desk, paperwork spread out on the table. There was nothing else in the room.

While she was still trying to absorb what was being said, Deuce appeared behind her.

Chantal looked at Deuce and then at Mary seeing the disbelief on their faces. It really was hard to digest. Then she looked back towards the desk.

It wasn't the man behind the desk that the three of them were staring at, it was the big concave window that took up the whole wall behind the desk that had their attention. She couldn't believe it. She was looking out at a world like she'd never seen.

There were multiple planets of different sizes and colors all close together, slowly rotating in their own individual orbits. Small specs that looked like shuttles or planes flew between them.

Earth Two? She looked back at the waterfall. Where was Gary? He was going to love this.

The End.

If you enjoyed this book, please take a moment to leave a review at Amazon or Goodreads and help spread the word.

Acknowledgment

I would like to thank Mark and Ken at Marken Performance in Kitchener, Ontario for all the work they have done on my special project. I'm really enjoying the '72 Corvette, and I think my brother would have too.

If you enjoyed this book, please take a moment to leave a review at <u>Goodreads</u> and help spread the word.

About the Author

Rejean Giguere is an avid outdoorsman, adventurer, photographer and artist. He enjoys fishing, hockey, golf, tennis, skiing and snowmobiling, his V-Max motorcycle and vintage Corvette.

He grew up in Canada and Europe, and enjoyed a business career in Toronto and Ottawa.

Visit his website at www.rejeangiguere.com